The Prince's Convenient Proposal

Barbara Hannay

HARLEQUIN® ROMANCE

Recycling programs for this product may not exist in your area.

ISBN-13: 978-0-373-74418-3

The Prince's Convenient Proposal

First North American Publication 2017

This edition published by arrangement with Harlequin Books S.A.

For questions and comments about the quality of this book, please contact us at CustomerService@Harlequin.com.

HARLEQUIN®
www.Harlequin.com

Printed in U.S.A.

Barbara Hannay has written over forty romance novels and has won a RITA® Award, an RT Reviewers' Choice Best Book Award and Australia's Romantic Book of the Year. A city-bred girl with a yen for country life, Barbara lives with her husband on a misty hillside in beautiful Far North Queensland, where they raise pigs and chickens and enjoy an untidy but productive garden.

Books by Barbara Hannay

Harlequin Romance

Bellaroo Creek!

Miracle in Bellaroo Creek

Changing Grooms

Runaway Bride

The Husband She'd Never Met
Falling for Mr. Mysterious
The Cattleman's Special Delivery
Second Chance with Her Soldier
A Very Special Holiday Gift

Visit the Author Profile page
at Harlequin.com for more titles.

CHAPTER ONE

WEDNESDAY MORNINGS WERE always quiet in the gallery, so any newcomer was bound to catch Charlie's eye as she sat patiently at the reception desk. This morning, her attention was certainly caught by the tall, dark-haired fellow who came striding through the arched doorway as if he owned the place. He was gobsmackingly handsome, but it was his commanding manner that made Charlie almost forget to offer him her customary, sunny and welcoming smile.

A serious mistake. The cut of this fellow's charcoal-grey suit suggested that he actually had the means to purchase one of the gallery's paintings.

And, boy, Charlie needed to sell a painting. Fast. Her father, Michael Morisset, was the artist most represented on these gallery walls and his finances were in dire straits. Again. Always.

Sadly, her charming and talented, but vague and impractical parent was hopeless with money. His finances had always been precarious, but until recently he and Charlie—actually, it had mostly been Charlie who'd struggled with this—had managed to make ends meet. Just. But now, her father had remarried and his new wife had produced a brand-new baby daughter, and his situation was even more desperate.

Charlie was thinking of Isla, her new, too fragile and tiny half-sister, as she flashed the newcomer a bright smile and lifted a catalogue brochure from the pile on the counter.

'Good morning,' she said warmly.

'Morning.' His response was cool, without any hint of an answering smile. His icy grey eyes narrowed as he stopped and stood very still, staring at Charlie.

She squeezed her facial muscles, forcing an even brighter smile as she held out a brochure. 'First time at the gallery, sir?'

Momentary surprise flashed in his eyes, but then he said, 'Of course.'

Charlie thought she caught the hint of an accent, and his gaze grew even chillier, which spoiled the handsome perfection of his cheekbones and jawline and thick, glossy dark hair.

'How are you, Olivia?' he asked.

Huh?

Charlie almost laughed. He looked so serious, but he was seriously deluded. 'I'm sorry. My name's not Olivia.'

The newcomer shook his head. 'Nice try.' He smiled this time, but the smile held no warmth. 'Don't play games. I've come a long way to find you, as you very well know.'

Now it was Charlie's turn to stare, while her mind raced. Was this fellow a loony? Should she call Security?

She glanced quickly around the gallery. A pair of elderly ladies were huddled at the far end of the large space, which had once been a warehouse. Their heads were together as they studied a Daphne Holden, a delicate water colour of a rose garden. The only other visitor, so far this morning, was the fellow in the chair by the window. He seemed to be asleep, most probably a homeless guy enjoying the air-conditioning.

At least no one was paying any attention to this weird conversation.

'I'm sorry,' Charlie said again. 'You're mistaken. My name is not Olivia. It's Charlie.'

His disbelief was instantly evident. In his eyes, in the curl of his lip.

'Charlotte, to be totally accurate,' she amended. 'Charlotte Morisset.' Again, she held out the catalogue. 'Would you like to see the gallery? We have some very fine—'

'No, I'm not interested in your paintings.' The man was clearly losing his patience. 'I haven't come to see the artwork. I don't know why you're doing this, Olivia, but whatever your reasons, the very least you owe me is an explanation.'

Charlie refused to apologise a second time. 'I told you, I'm not—' She stopped in mid-sentence. There was little to be gained by repeating her claim. She was tempted to reach for her handbag, to show this arrogant so and so her driver's licence and to prove she wasn't this Olivia chick. But she had no idea if she could trust this man. For all she knew, this could be some kind of trap. He could be trying to distract her while thieves crept in to steal the paintings.

Or perhaps she'd been watching too much television?

She was rather relieved when a middle-aged couple came into the gallery, all smiles. She always greeted gallery visitors warmly, and Grim Face had no choice but to wait his turn as she bestowed this couple with an extra-sunny smile and handed them each a catalogue.

'We're particularly interested in Michael Morisset,' the man said.

Wonderful! 'We have an excellent collection of his paintings.' Charlie tried not to sound too pleased and eager. 'The Morrisets are mostly on this nearest wall.' She waved towards the collection of her father's bold, dramatic oils depicting so many facets of Sydney's inner-city landscape. 'You'll find them all listed in the catalogue.'

'And they're all for sale?' asked the woman.

'Except for the few samples of his earliest work from the nineteen-eighties. It's all explained in the catalogue, but if you have any questions, please don't hesitate to ask me. That's why I'm here.'

'Wonderful. Thank you.'

The couple continued to smile broadly and they looked rather excited as they moved away. Behind her back, Charlie crossed her fingers. Her father needed a big sale so badly.

Unfortunately Grim Face was still hanging around, and now he leaned towards her. 'You do an excellent Australian accent, but you can't keep it up. I've found you now, Olivia, and I won't be leaving until we have this sorted.'

'There's nothing to sort.' Charlie felt a stirring of panic. 'You've made a mistake and that's all there is to it. I don't even *know* anyone called Olivia.' She sent a frantic glance to the couple studying her father's paintings.

After she'd given them enough time to have a good look, she would approach them with her gentle sales pitch. Today she had to be extra careful to hit the right note—she mustn't be too cautious, or too pushy—and she really needed this guy out of her hair.

She cut her gaze from his, as if their conversation was ended, and made a show of tidying the brochures before turning to her computer screen.

'When do you get time off for lunch?' he asked.

Charlie stiffened. He was really annoying her. And worrying her. Was he some kind of stalker? And anyway, she didn't take 'time off for lunch'. She ate a sandwich and made a cup of tea in the tiny office off this reception area, but she wasn't about to share that information with this jerk.

'I'm afraid I'm here all day,' she replied with an imperiousness that almost matched his.

'Then I'll see you at six when the gallery closes.'

Charlie opened her mouth to protest when he cut her off with a raised hand.

'And don't try anything foolish, like trying to slip away again. My men will be watching you.'

His *men*?

What the hell…?

Truly appalled, Charlie pulled her handbag from under the desk, dumped it on the counter, and ferociously yanked the zipper. 'Listen, mate, I'll prove to you that I'm not this Olivia person.' Pulling out her purse, she flipped it open to reveal her driver's licence. 'My name's Charlotte Morisset. Like it or lump it.'

Her pulse was racketing at a giddy pace as he

leaned forward to inspect the proffered licence. There was something very not right about this. He had the outward appearance of a highly successful man. Handsome and well groomed, with that shiny dark hair and flashing grey eyes, he might have been a male model or a film star, or even a barrister. A federal politician. Someone used to being in the spotlight.

It made no sense that he would confuse her—ordinary, everyday Charlie Morisset from the wrong end of Bankstown—with anyone from his circle.

Unless he was a high-class criminal. Perhaps he'd heard the recent ripples in the art world. Perhaps he knew that her father was on the brink of finally garnering attention for his work.

My men will be watching you.

Charlie snapped her purse shut, hoping he hadn't had time to read her address and date of birth.

'So you've changed your name, but not your date of birth,' he said with just a hint of menace.

Charlie let out a huff—half sigh, half terror. 'Listen, mister. I want you to leave. Now. If you don't, I'm calling the police.' She reached for the phone.

As she did so Grim Face slipped a hand into the breast pocket of his coat.

White-hot fear strafed through Charlie. He

was getting out his gun. Her hands were shaking as she pressed triple zero. But it was probably too late. She was about to die.

Instead of producing a gun, however, he slapped a photograph down on the counter. 'This is the girl I'm looking for.' He eyed Charlie with the steely but watchful gaze of a detective ready to pounce. 'Her name is Olivia Belaire.'

Once again, Charlie gasped.

It was the photo that shocked her this time. It was a head and shoulders photograph of herself.

There could be no doubt. That was her face. Those were her unruly blonde curls, her blue eyes, her too-wide mouth. Even the dimple in the girl's right cheek was the same shape as hers.

Charlie heard a voice speaking from her phone, asking whether she wanted the police, the ambulance or the fire brigade.

'Ah, no,' she said quickly. 'Sorry, I'm OK. It was a false alarm.'

As she disconnected, she stared at the photo. Every detail was exact, including the tilt of the girl's smile. Except no, wait a minute, this dimple was in the girl's left cheek.

Then again, Charlie supposed some cameras might reverse the image.

The girl, who looked exactly like her and was supposed to be Olivia Belaire, was even wearing a plain white T-shirt, just as Charlie was now, tucked into blue jeans. And there was a beach in the background, which could easily have been Sydney's Bondi Beach. Charlie tried to remember what she'd been wearing the last time she'd been to Bondi.

'Where'd you get this photo?'

For the first time, Grim Face almost smiled. 'I took it with my own camera, as you know very well. At Saint-Tropez.'

Charlie rubbed at her forehead, wishing that any part of this made sense. She swallowed, staring hard at the photo. 'Who is this girl? How do you know her?'

His jaw tightened with impatience. 'It's time to stop the games now, Olivia.'

'I'm not—' This was getting tedious. 'What's *your* name?' she asked instead. 'What's this all about?'

Now it was his turn to sigh, to give a weary, resigned shake of his head and to run a frustrated hand through his thick dark hair, ruffling it rather attractively.

Charlie found herself watching with inappropriate interest.

'My name's Rafe.' He sounded bored, as if he was repeating something she already knew. 'Short for Rafael. Rafael St Romain.'

'Sorry, that doesn't ring a bell. It sounds—maybe—French?'

'French is our national language,' the man called Rafe acceded. 'Although most of our citizens also speak English. I live in Montaigne.'

'That cute little country in the Alps?'

He continued to look bored, as if he was sure she was playing with him. 'Exactly.'

Charlie had heard about Montaigne, of course. It was very small and not especially important, as far as she could tell, but it was famous for skiing and—and for something else, something glamorous like jewellery.

She'd seen photos in magazines of celebrities, even royalty, holidaying there. 'Well, that's very interesting, Rafe, but it doesn't—'

Charlie paused. Damn. She couldn't afford to waste time with this distraction. She made a quick check around the gallery. The vagrant was still asleep in the window seat. The old ladies were having a good old chinwag. The other couple were also deep in discussion, still looking at her father's paintings and studying the catalogue.

She needed to speak to them. She had a feeling they were on the verge of making a purchase and she couldn't afford to let them slip away, to 'think things over'.

'I *really* don't have time for this,' she told Rafael St Romain.

Out of the corner of her eye, she was aware of the couple nodding together, as if they'd reached a decision. Ignoring his continuing grim expression, she skirted the counter and stepped out into the gallery, her soft-soled shoes silent on the tiles.

'What did you think of the Morissets?' she asked, directing her question to the couple.

They looked up and she sent them an encouraging smile.

'The paintings are wonderful,' the man said. 'So bold and original.'

'We'd love one for our lounge room,' added the woman.

Her husband nodded. 'We're just trying to make a decision.'

'We need to go home and take another look at our wall space,' the woman said quickly.

Charlie's heart sank. She knew from experience that the chances of this couple returning to make an actual purchase were slim. Most true art lovers knew exactly what they wanted as soon as they saw it.

This couple were more interested in interior décor. Already they were walking away.

The woman's smile was almost apologetic, as she looked back over her shoulder, as if she'd guessed that they'd disappointed Charlie. 'We'll see you soon,' she called.

Charlie smiled and nodded, but as they disappeared through the doorway her shoulders drooped.

She wished this weren't her problem, but, even though she'd moved out of home into a tiny shoebox studio flat when her father remarried, she still looked after her father's finances. It was a task she'd assumed at the age of fourteen, making sure that the rent and the bills were paid while she did her best to discourage her dad from throwing too many overly extravagant parties, or from taking expensive holidays to 'fire up his muse'.

Unfortunately, her new stepmother, Skye, was as unworldly and carefree as her dad, so she'd been happy to leave this task in Charlie's hands. The bills all came to the gallery and Charlie was already trying to figure out how she'd pay the electricity bills for this month, as well as providing the funds for nourishing meals.

Skye would need plenty of nourishment while she cared for Isla, *tiny* little Isla who'd taken a scarily long time to start breathing after she was born. Despite her small size, Charlie's baby sister had looked perfect, though, with the sweetest cap of dark hair, a neat nose and darling little mouth like a rosebud. Perfect tiny fingers and toes.

But the doctors were running some tests on Isla. Charlie wasn't sure what they were looking for, but the thought that something might be wrong with her baby sister was terrifying. Since Isla's birth, her father had more or less lived at the hospital, camping by Skye's bed.

Charlie was dragged from these gloomy thoughts by the phone ringing. She turned back to the counter, annoyed to see that Rafael St Romain in his expensive grey suit hadn't budged an inch. And he was still watching her.

Deliberately not meeting his distrustful grey gaze, she picked up the phone.

'Charlie?'

She knew immediately from the tone of her father's voice that he was worried. A chill shimmied through her. 'Hi.' She turned her back on the exquisitely suited Rafael.

'We've had some bad news about Isla,' her father said. 'There's a problem with her heart.'

Horrified, Charlie sank forward, elbows supporting her on the counter. *Her heart.* 'How—how bad is it?'

'Bad.'

Sickening dizziness swept over Charlie. 'What can they do?'

There was silence on the other end of the phone.

'Dad?'

'The doctors here can't do anything. Her problem is very rare and complicated. You should see her, Charlie. She's in isolation, with tubes everywhere and all these monitors.' Her father's voice was ragged and Charlie knew he was only just holding himself together.

'Surely they can do *something*?'

'It doesn't sound like it, but there's a cardiologist in Boston who's had some success with surgery.'

'Boston!' Charlie bit back a groan. Her mind raced. A surgeon in Boston meant serious money. Mountains of it. Poor little Isla. What could they do?

Charlie knew only too well that her father had little chance of raising a quick loan for this vital operation. He'd never even been able to raise a mortgage. His income flow was so erratic, the banks wouldn't take the risk.

Poor Isla. What on earth could they do? Charlie looked again at the paintings hanging on the walls. She knew they were good. And since her father had married Skye, there'd been a new confidence in his work, a new daring. His latest stuff had shown a touch of genius.

Charlie was sure Michael Morisset was on the very edge of being discovered by the world and becoming famous. But it would be too late for Isla.

'I'm going to ring around,' her father said. 'To see what help I can get. You never know...'

'Yes, that's a good idea,' Charlie told him fervently. 'Good luck. I'll make some calls too and see what I can do. Even if I can get some advice, anything that might help.'

'That would be great, love. Thanks.'

'I'll call again later.'

'OK.'

'Give Skye a hug from me.'

Charlie disconnected, set the phone down, and let her head sink into her hands as she wrestled with the unbearable thought of her newborn baby sister's tiny damaged heart, the poor, precious creature struggling to hold on to her fragile new life.

'Excuse me.'

She jumped as the deep masculine voice intruded into her misery. She'd forgotten all about Rafael St Romain and his stupid photo. Swiping at tears, she turned to him. 'I'm sorry. I don't have time to deal with this Olivia business.'

'Yes, I can see that.'

To her surprise he seemed less formidable. Perhaps he'd overheard her end of the conversation. He almost looked concerned.

'You were speaking with your father,' he said.

Charlie's chin lifted. 'Yes.' Not that it was any of his business.

'Then clearly I am in the wrong. I apologise. The woman I'm searching for has no father.'

'Right. Good.' At least he would leave her in peace now.

'But the likeness is uncanny,' he said.

'It is.' Charlie couldn't deny this. The photo that had supposedly been taken in Saint-Tropez showed a mirror image of herself, and, despite her new worries about Isla, she couldn't help being curious. 'How do you know this Olivia?' she found herself asking. 'Who is she?'

Rafael regarded her steadily and he took a nerve-racking age before he answered. Trapped in his powerful gaze, Charlie flashed hot and cold. The man was ridiculously attractive. Under different circumstances she might have been quite helplessly smitten.

Instead, she merely felt discomfited. And annoyed.

'Olivia Belaire is my fiancée,' he said at last. 'And for the sake of my country's future, I have to find her.'

For the sake of his country's future?

Charlie's jaw was already gaping and couldn't drop any further. This surprise, coming on top of her father's bombshell, was almost too much to take in.

How was it possible that a girl who looked *exactly* the same as herself could live on the other side of the world and somehow be responsible for an entire country's future?

Who was Olivia?

Charlie had heard of doppelgängers, but she'd never really believed they existed in real life.

But what other explanation could there be?

A twin sister?

This thought was barely formed before fine hairs lifted on Charlie's skin. And before she could call a halt to her thoughts, they galloped on at a reckless pace.

This girl, Olivia, had no father, while to all intents and purposes she, Charlie, had no mother.

Charlie's father had always been vague about her mother. Her parents had divorced when Charlie was a baby and her mother had taken off for Europe, never to be heard from or seen again. Over the years, Charlie had sometimes fretted over her mother's absence, but she and her dad had been so close, he'd made up for the loss. Money worries aside, he'd been a wonderful dad.

The two of them had enjoyed many fabulous adventures together, sailing in the South Pacific, hiking in Nepal, living in the middle of rice fields in Bali while her father taught English during the day and painted at night. They'd also had a few very exciting months in New York.

When her father had married Skye, Charlie had been happy to see him so settled at last, and she'd been thrilled when Skye became pregnant. She liked the idea of being part of a bigger family. Now, though, she couldn't help thinking back and wondering why her father had limited his travels to Asia, strictly avoiding Europe. Had he actually been avoiding her mother?

Charlie gulped at the next thought. Had he been afraid that she'd discover her twin sister?

Surely not.

CHAPTER TWO

RAFE WAS REELING as he watched the play of emotions on the girl's face. He was still coming to terms with the frustrating reality that this wasn't Olivia, but her exact double, Charlotte.

Charlie.

The likeness to his missing fiancée was incredible. No wonder his detectives had been fooled. The resemblance went beyond superficial features such as Charlie Morisset's golden curls and blue eyes and her neatly curving figure. It was there in the way she moved, in the tilt of her chin, in the spirited flash in her eyes.

Take away her blue jeans and sneakers and put her in an *haute couture* gown and, apart from her Australian accent, which wasn't too terribly broad, no one in Montaigne would ever tell the difference.

The possibilities presented by this resemblance were so tempting.

Rafe, Crown Prince of Montaigne, needed a fiancée.

He'd been engaged for barely a fortnight before Olivia Belaire took flight. Admittedly, his arrangement with Olivia had been one of hasty convenience rather than romance. They'd struck a business deal in fact, and Rafe understood that Olivia might well have panicked when she'd come to terms with the realities of being married to a prince with enormous responsibilities.

Rafe had come close to panicking, too. One minute he'd been an AWOL playboy prince, travelling the world, enjoying a delightful and endless series of parties…in Los Angeles, London, Dubai, Monaco…with an endless stream of girls to match…redheads, brunettes, blondes… all long-legged and glamorous and willing.

For years, especially in the years since his mother's death, Rafe had been flying high. He and Sheikh Faysal Daood Taariq, his best friend from university, had been A-list invitees at all the most glittering celebrity parties. As was their custom, they'd made quite a hit when they arrived at the wild party in Saint-Tropez.

Just a few short weeks ago.

Such a shock it had been that night, in the midst of the glitz and glamour, for Rafe to receive a phone call from home.

He'd been flirting outrageously with Olivia Belaire, and the girl was dancing barefoot while Rafe drank champagne from one of her shoes, when a white-coated waiter had tugged at his elbow.

'Excuse me, Your Highness, you're needed on the phone.'

'Not now,' Rafe had responded, waving the fellow off with the champagne-filled shoe. 'I'm busy.'

'I'm sorry, sir, but it's a phone call from Montaigne. From the castle. They said it's urgent.'

'No, no, no,' Rafe had insisted rather tipsily. 'Nothing's so important that it can't wait till morning.'

'It's urgent news about your father, Your Highness.'

In an instant Rafe had sobered. In fact, his veins had turned to ice as he'd walked stiff-backed to the phone to receive the news that his father, the robust and popular ruling Prince of Montaigne, had died suddenly of a heart attack.

Rafe's memories of the rest of that dreadful night were a blur. He'd been shocked and grief-stricken and filled with remorse, and he'd spent half of the night on the phone, talking to castle staff, to his country's Chancellor, to Montaigne's Chief of Intelligence, to his father's secretary, his father's publicist—who were now Rafe's secretary and publicist.

There'd been so much that he'd had to come to terms with in a matter of hours, including the horrifying, inescapable fact that he needed to find a fiancée in a hurry.

An ancient clause in Montaigne's constitution required a crown prince to be married, or at least betrothed, within two days of a ruling prince's death. The subsequent marriage must take place within two months of this date.

Such a disaster!

The prospect of a sudden marriage had appalled Rafe. He'd been free for so long, he'd never considered settling down with one woman. Or at least, no single woman had ever sufficiently snagged his attention to the point that he'd considered a permanent relationship.

Suddenly, however, his country's future was at stake.

Looking back on the past couple of weeks, Rafe was ashamed to admit that he'd been only dimly aware of the mining company that threatened Montaigne. But on that harrowing night he'd been forced to pay attention.

The message was clear. Without a fiancée, Rafe St Romain would be deposed as Prince of Montaigne, the Chancellor would take control and the mongrels intent on his country's ruin would have their way. In a blink they would tie up the rights to the mineral wealth hidden deep within Montaigne's Alps.

Among the many briefings Rafe had received

that night, he'd been given an alarming warning from Montaigne's Chief of Intelligence.

'You cannot trust your Chancellor, Claude Pontier. We are certain he's corrupt, but we're still working on ways to prove it. We don't have enough information yet, but Pontier has links to the Leroy Mining Company.'

In other words…if Rafe wasn't married within the required time frame, he would be deposed and the Chancellor could take control, allowing the greedy pack of miners to cause irreparable damage to Montaigne. Given free rein, they would heartlessly tear the mountains apart, wreaking havoc on his country's beautiful landscape and totally destroying the economy based on centuries-old traditions.

With only two days to produce a fiancée, Rafe had turned to the nearest available girl, who had happened to be the extraordinarily pretty, but slightly vacuous, Olivia Belaire. Unfortunately, less than two weeks after their spectacular and very public engagement ball, Olivia had done a runner.

To an extent, Rafe could sympathise with Olivia. The night she'd agreed to step up as his fiancée had been a crazy whirlwind, and she certainly hadn't had time to fully take in the deeper ramifications of marriage to a ruling prince. But Rafe had paid her an exceedingly generous amount, and the terms for their eventual divorce were unstinting, so he found it hard to remain sympathetic now, when his country's problems were so dire.

Despite his wayward playboy history, Rafe loved his country with all his heart and he loved the people of Montaigne, who were almost as famous for the exquisite jewellery they made from locally sourced gemstones as they were for their wonderful alpine cuisine. With the addition of the country's world-class ski slopes, Montaigne offered an exclusive tourist package that had been his country's lifeblood since the eighteenth century.

Montaigne could never survive the invasion of these miners.

Regrettably, his police still hadn't enough evidence to pin Pontier down. They needed more time. And Rafe desperately needed a fiancée.

Damn it, if Charlie Morisset hadn't just received a phone call from her father that had clearly distressed her, Rafe would have proposed that she fly straight home with him. She would be the perfect foil, a lifesaving stand-in until Olivia was unearthed and placated, and reinstated as his fiancée. He would pay Charlie handsomely, of course.

It seemed, however, that Charlie was dealing with some kind of family crisis of her own, so this probably wasn't the choice moment to crassly wave money in her face in the hope that he could whisk her away.

'How on earth did you manage to lose Olivia?'

Rafe frowned at Charlie's sudden, cheekily posed question.

'Did you frighten her off?' she asked, blue eyes blazing. 'You didn't hurt her, did you?'

Rafe was almost too affronted to answer. 'Of course I didn't hurt her.' In truth, he'd barely touched her.

Instantly sobered by the news of his father's death, he had dropped his playboy persona the very moment he and Olivia had left the party in Saint-Tropez. As they'd hurried back to Montaigne, Rafe had reverted to the perfect gentlemanly Prince. Apart from the few tipsy kisses they'd exchanged while they'd danced at the party, he'd barely laid a hand on the girl.

Of course, he'd been grateful to Olivia for agreeing to a hasty marriage of convenience, but since then he'd been busy dealing with formalities and his father's funeral and his own sudden responsibilities.

'I'm sorry to have troubled you,' he told Charlie now with icy politeness.

She gave a distracted nod.

He took a step back, loath to let go of this

lifeline, but fearing he had little choice. Charlie Morisset was clearly absorbed by her own worries.

'I think Olivia might be my sister,' she said.

Rafe stilled. 'Is there a chance?'

She nodded. 'I know that my mother lives somewhere in Europe. I—I've never met her. Well, not that I remember—'

Her lower lip trembled ever so slightly, and the tough, don't-mess-with-me edge that Rafe had sensed in Charlie from the outset disappeared. Now she looked suddenly vulnerable, almost childlike.

To his dismay, he felt his heart twist.

'I've met Olivia's mother,' he said. 'Her name is Vivian. Vivian Belaire.'

'Oh.' Charlie looked as suddenly pale and upset as she had when she was speaking to her father on the phone. She seemed to sag in the middle, as if her knees were in danger of giving way. 'That was my mother's name,' she said faintly. 'Vivian.'

Rafe had been on the point of departure, but now, as Charlie sank onto a stool and let out a heavy sigh, he stood his ground.

'I didn't know she had another daugh—' Charlie swallowed. 'What's she like? My mother?'

Rafe was remembering the suntanned, platinum blonde with the hard eyes and the paunchy billionaire husband, who'd had way too many drinks at the engagement ball.

'She has fair hair, like yours,' he said. 'She's—attractive. I'm afraid I don't know her very well.'

'I had no idea I had a sister. I knew nothing about Olivia.'

He wondered if this was an opening. Was there still a chance to state his case?

'I can't believe my father never told me about her.' Charlie closed her eyes and pressed her fingers to her temples as if a headache was starting.

Then she straightened suddenly, opened her eyes and flashed him a guilty grimace. 'I can't deal with this now. I have other problems, way more important.'

Disappointed, Rafe accepted this with a dignified bow. 'Thanks for your time,' he said politely. 'I hope your other problems are quickly sorted.'

'Thank you.' Charlie dropped her gaze to her phone and began to scroll through numbers.

Rafe turned to leave. This dash to the southern hemisphere had been a fruitless exercise, a waste of precious time. His detectives would have to work doubly hard now to find Olivia.

'But maybe I *could* see you this evening.'

Charlie's voice brought him whirling round.

She looked rather forlorn and very *alone* as she stood at the counter, phone in hand. To Rafe's dismay her eyes were glittering with tears.

So different from the tough little terrier who'd barked at him when he first arrived in her gallery.

Maybe I could see you this evening.

He wasn't planning to hang around here till this evening. If Charlie couldn't help him, he would leave Sydney as soon as his private jet was available for take-off.

But the news of her mother and sister had clearly rocked her, and it had come on top of a distressing phone call from her father. With some reluctance, Rafe couldn't deny that he was part-way responsible for Charlie's pain. And he couldn't stifle a small skerrick of hope.

He was running out of time. If this was a dead end, he needed to hurry home, but if there was even a slight chance that she could help…

'I've got the gallery to run and some important family business to sort out,' Charlie said self-importantly. 'But I'd like to know more about Olivia. Maybe we could grab a very quick coffee?'

Was it worth the bother of wasting precious hours for a very quick coffee? The chances of persuading this girl to take off with him were microscopic.

But what other options did he have? Olivia had well and truly gone to ground.

Rafe heard himself saying, 'I could come back here at six.'

Charlie nodded. 'Right, then. Let's do that.'

By the end of the day, Charlie was feeling quite desperate. Her phone calls hadn't produced promising results. Apart from launching a *Save Isla* charity fund, she didn't have too many options. When she called her father she learned that he hadn't fared any better.

After her very quick meeting with Rafe, she and her father planned to meet to discuss strategies, and Charlie knew she would be up all night, setting up a website and a special Facebook page, and responding to the media outlets she'd contacted during the day.

Unfortunately, there would be no time to challenge her father about Olivia. Charlie was deeply hurt that he'd never told her about her twin sister, but right now she had another sister to worry about, and she knew her dad was beside himself with worry. It was totally the wrong time to pester him about Olivia Belaire.

Promptly at six, Rafe was waiting at the gallery's front door. To Charlie's surprise, he'd changed into a black T-shirt and jeans, and the casual look, complete with a five o'clock shadow and windblown hair, made him look less like a corporate raider and more like—

Gulp.

The man of her dreams.

She quickly knocked that thought on the head. She was already regretting her impulsive request to see him again. There was little she could learn about Olivia over a quick cup of coffee. But Charlie needed to understand why her sister might have agreed to marry such a compellingly attractive guy and then run away from him.

It was bad enough having one sister to worry about. She needed Rafe to set her mind at rest, so she could channel all her attention to Isla's cause.

Suddenly having two sisters, both of them in trouble, was hard to wrap her head around. As for her emotions, she'd have to sort them out later. Right now, she was running on pure adrenaline.

In no time, Charlie and Rafe were seated in a booth in the café around the corner, which was now packed with the after-work crowd. The smell of coffee and Greek pastry filled the small but popular space and they had to lean close to be heard above the noisy chatter.

'We should have gone back to my hotel,' Rafe said, scowling at the crowded booths.

'No,' Charlie responded quite definitely.

'It would have been quieter.'

'But it would have taken time. Time I don't have.'

His eyes narrowed as he watched her, but he'd lost the hawk-eyed detective look. Now he just looked extraordinarily *hot*, and she found herself fighting the tingles and flashes his proximity caused.

Their coffees arrived. A tiny cup of espresso for Rafe and a mug of frothy cappuccino for Charlie, as well as a serving of baklava. Charlie's tummy rumbled at the sight of the flaky filo pastry layered with cinnamon-spiced nut filling. Rafe had declared that he wasn't hungry, but she wasn't prepared to hold back. This would probably be the only meal she'd have time for this evening.

She scooped a creamy dollop of froth from the top of her mug. 'So, the thing I need to know, Rafe, is why my sister ran away from you.'

He smiled. It was only a faint smile, but enough to light up his grey eyes in ways that made Charlie feel slightly breathless. 'I'm afraid I can't answer that,' he said. 'She didn't leave an explanation.'

'But something must have happened. Did you have a row?'

'Not at all. Our relationship was very—' He paused as if he was searching for the right word. 'Very civilised.'

Charlie thought this was a strange word to describe a romantic liaison. Where was the soppiness? The passion? She imagined that getting engaged to a man like Rafe would involve a truckload of passion.

Even so, she found herself believing him when he said he hadn't hurt Olivia. 'So you've heard nothing,' she said. 'You must be terribly worried.'

'I have received a postcard,' said Rafe. 'There were no postage marks. The card was hand delivered, but unfortunately no one realised the significance until it was too late. It simply said that Olivia was fine and she was sorry.'

'Oh.' Charlie offered him an awkward smile of sympathy. No matter what reasons Olivia had for wanting to get out of the engagement, she'd been flaky to just take off, without facing up to Rafe with a proper explanation.

'My mother ran away,' she told him, overlooking the hurt this admission made.

Rafe lifted one dark eyebrow. 'Do you think Olivia might have inherited an escapee gene?'

Charlie was sure he hadn't meant this seriously, but the mere mention of inheritance and genes reminded her of Isla. She had to make this conversation quick, so she could get on with more important matters. 'Look,' she said, frowning, to let him know she was serious. 'I'd really like to know a little more about my sister. Where did you meet her?'

'In Saint-Tropez. At a party.'

'So, she's—well off?'

'Her father—her mother's husband,' Rafe corrected, 'is an extremely wealthy businessman. They have a house in the French Riviera and another in Switzerland, and I think there might also be a holiday house in America.'

'Wow.' *And my father can't even afford to buy one house.* Charlie tried to imagine her sister's life. 'Does she have a job?'

'None that I know of.'

'So, how does she spend her days?'

'Her days?' Rafe's lip curled in a slightly bitter smile. 'Olivia's not exactly a daytime sort of person. She's more of a night owl.'

Charlie blinked at this. She only had the vaguest notions of life on the French Riviera. She supposed Olivia was part of the jet-set who spent their time partying and shopping for clothes. If she emerged in the daylight, it was probably to lie in the sun, working hard on her suntan. Just the same, it bothered her that Rafe wasn't speaking about her sister with any sense of deep fondness. 'And what sort of work do you do?' she asked.

'That's a complicated question.'

She felt a burst of impatience. 'I don't have much time.'

'Then I'll cut to the chase. I'm my country's ruler.'

Charlie stared at him, mouth gaping, as she struggled to take this in. 'A ruler? Like—like a king?'

'Montaigne's only a small principality, but yes.' His voice dropped as if he didn't wish to be overheard. 'I'm the Prince of Montaigne. Prince Rafael the Third, to be exact.'

'Holy—' Just in time, Charlie cut off a swear word. She couldn't believe she'd met a real live prince and was sitting in her local café with him. Couldn't believe that her sister had actually scored a prince as a fiancé. 'You mean I should be calling you Sir, or Your Highness, or something?'

Rafe smiled. 'Please, no. Rafe's fine.'

Almost immediately, another thought struck Charlie. 'Olivia might have been abducted, mightn't she? That postcard might have been a—a hoax.'

Rafe shook his head. 'Security footage in the castle shows her leaving of her own volition.

We know she drove her car towards Grenoble. After that—?' He frowned. 'She disappeared.'

'She might have been kidnapped.'

'There's been no request for a ransom.'

'Right.' Charlie gave a helpless shrug. 'And you've had your people searching everywhere? Even down here in Australia?'

'Yes.'

As Charlie sipped her coffee, she tried to put herself in Olivia Belaire's shoes. What would it be like to be engaged to this good-looking Prince? To be marrying into royalty? Would Olivia have been expected to undertake a host of public duties? Would she be required to chair meetings? Run charities? Visit the children's hospital?

At the very thought of a children's hospital, she shivered. *Poor little Isla.*

Fascinating though this conversation was, she'd have to cut it short.

But, as she speared a piece of baklava with her fork, she couldn't help asking, 'Do you think Olivia might have got cold feet? Could she have been worried about the whole royalty thing? All the responsibilities?'

'It's possible.'

'That's hard on you, Rafe. I—I'm sorry.' Lowering the enticing pastry to her plate, Charlie picked up her phone instead. She needed to check the time. She had to meet her father. She really should leave.

As if he sensed this, Rafe said, 'Before you go, I have a proposition.'

'No way,' Charlie said quickly, suddenly nervous. Prince or not, she'd only just met the man and she wasn't about to become embroiled in his troubles. She had enough of her own.

'You could earn a great deal of money,' he said.

Now he had her attention.

CHAPTER THREE

CHARLIE CERTAINLY BRIGHTENED at the mention of money, and Rafe was surprised by his stab of disappointment. After all, her reaction was exactly what he'd expected.

Now, however, caution also showed in Charlie's expressive face, and that was also to be expected.

'Why would you offer me money?' she asked.

'To entice you to stand in as your sister.'

She stared at him as if he'd grown an extra head. 'You've got to be joking.'

'I'm perfectly serious.'

Leaning back, she continued to watch him with obvious distrust. 'You want me to pretend to be your fiancée?'

'Yes.'

'Oh, for heaven's sake, that's ridiculous. Why?'

At least, she listened without interrupting while he explained. She leaned forward again, elbows on the table, chin resting in one hand, blue eyes intent, listening as if transfixed. Rafe told her about the inconvenient clause in Montaigne's constitution, about the country's mineral wealth and the very real threat of a takeover, and the possibility of ruin for the people who meant so much to him.

Charlie didn't speak when he finished. She sat for a minute or two, staring first at him and then into space with a small furrow between her neatly arched brows. Then she picked up her phone.

'Excuse me,' she said without looking up from the small screen. 'I'm just researching you.'

Rafe smiled. 'Of course.' He drained his coffee and sat back, waiting with barely restrained patience. But despite his tension, he thought how pleasant it was to be in a country where almost nobody knew him. Of course, his bodyguards were positioned just outside the café, but in every other way he was just an ordinary customer in a small Sydney coffee shop, chatting with a very pretty girl. The anonymity was a luxury he rarely enjoyed.

'Wow,' Charlie said, looking up from her phone. 'You're the real deal.'

Rafe's moment of fantasy was over. 'So,' he said. 'Would you consider my proposal?'

She grimaced. 'I hate to sound mercenary, but how much money are we talking about?'

'Two hundred and fifty thousand dollars US.'

Charlie's eyes almost popped out of her head. Her first instinct was to say no, she couldn't possibly consider accepting such a sum. But then she remembered Isla.

Fanning her face with her hand, she took several deep breaths before she answered. 'Crikey, Rafe, you sure know how to tempt a girl.'

Wow—not only would she be able to help Isla, she would be a step closer to finding out about Olivia as well. How could she pass up such an opportunity to meet her long-lost sister and maybe get some answers?

But even as she played with these beguiling possibilities Charlie gave Rafe a rueful smile. 'It wouldn't work, though, would it? I'd give the game away as soon as I arrived in Montaigne and opened my mouth.'

Yes, her Aussie accent *was* a problem. 'Do you speak French?'

'Oui.'

'You learnt French here in Australia?' Rafe asked in French.

'I went to school in New Caledonia,' Charlie replied with quite a passable French accent. 'I lived there for a few years with my father. Our teacher was a proper Frenchwoman. Mademoiselle Picard.'

Rafe smiled with relief. Charlie's French

might be limited, but she could probably get by. 'I think you would manage well enough. Olivia isn't a native French speaker.'

'As long as I dropped the crikeys?'

His smile deepened. 'That would certainly help, but we would try to limit the amount of time you needed to speak in public. It's all about appearances, really. And when it comes to how you look, you certainly had me and my detectives fooled.'

'But I haven't agreed to this,' Charlie said quickly. 'It's so risky. I mean, there's so much room for things to go wrong. What will happen, for example, if Olivia doesn't turn up before your cut-off date? *I* couldn't possibly marry you.'

She went bright pink as she said this.

Rafe watched the rosy tide with fascination. This girl was such a beguiling mix of innocence and worldliness. But now wasn't the time to be distracted.

'I'm confident we'll find Olivia,' he assured her. 'But whatever happens, you have my word. If you come to Montaigne with me, you'll be free to leave at the end of the month, if not sooner.'

'Hmm… What about—?' Charlie looked embarrassed. 'You—you wouldn't expect me to actually behave like a fiancée, would you? In private, I mean?'

This time Rafe manfully held back his urge to smile. 'Are you worried that I'd expect to ravish you on a nightly basis?'

'No, of course not.' She dropped her gaze to the half-eaten baklava on her plate. 'Well, yes… perhaps. I guess…'

'There's no need to worry,' he said more gently. 'Again, you have my word, Charlie. If you agreed to this, I would proudly escort you to public appearances as my fiancée, but in both public and in private I'd be a total gentleman. You'd have your own suite of rooms in the castle.'

Just the same, the thought of taking Charlie to bed was tempting. Extremely so. Despite her innocent, cautious façade, Rafe sensed an exciting wildness in her, an essential spark he'd found lacking in her sister.

But, sadly, his years as a playboy prince were behind him. Now responsibility for his country weighed heavily. If Charlie agreed to return with him to Montaigne, the engagement would be a purely political, diplomatic exercise, just as it had been with Olivia.

Charlie was very quiet now, as if she was giving his proposal serious thought.

'So what do you think?' he couldn't help prompting, while trying desperately to keep the impatience from his voice.

Charlie looked up at him, all big blue eyes and dark lashes, and he could see her internal battle as she weighed up the pros and cons.

Rafe wished he understood those cons. Was she worried about leaving her job at short notice? Were there family commitments? Did this involve the phone call from her father? A jealous lover?

He frowned at this last possibility. But surely, if there was a serious boyfriend on the scene, Charlie would have mentioned him by now.

'I can't pretend I'm not interested, Rafe,' she said suddenly. 'But I need to talk to—to someone.'

So...perhaps there was a boyfriend, after all. Rafe tried not to frown.

'When do you need a decision?' she asked.

'As soon as possible. I hoped to fly out tonight.'

'Tonight? Can you book a flight that quickly?'

'I don't need to book. I have a private jet.'

'Of course you do,' Charlie said softly and she rolled her eyes to the ceiling. 'You're a prince.' She gave a slow, disbelieving shake of her head, but then her gaze was direct as she met his. 'What time do you want to leave, then?' she asked.

Now. 'Ten o'clock? Eleven at the latest.' He pulled a chequebook from his pocket and filled in the necessary details, including his scrawled signature. 'Take this with you,' he said as he tore off the cheque.

Charlie took it gingerly, almost as if it were a time bomb. She swallowed as she stared at it. 'You'd hand over that amount of money? Just like that? You trust me?'

Rafe didn't like to point out that his men would be tailing her, so he simply nodded.

She folded the cheque and slipped it into her handbag and she looked pale as she rose from her seat. 'I'll be as quick as I can,' she said. 'Give me your phone number and I'll text you.'

CHAPTER FOUR

MICHAEL MORISSET, WHO had the same curls and clear blue eyes that Charlie had inherited, looked as if he'd aged ten years when she met him at the hospital.

It was frightening to see her normally upbeat and carefree father looking so haggard and worn.

Skye looked even worse. Only a few short days ago, the happy mother had been glowing as she proudly showed off her sweet newborn daughter. Now Skye looked pale and gaunt, with huge dark circles under her eyes. Her shoulders were stooped and even her normally glossy auburn hair hung in limp strands to her shoulders.

Charlie's eyes stung as she hugged her stepmother. She couldn't imagine how terrified Skye must be to know that her sweet little daughter had only the most tenuous hold on life.

'Would you like to see Isla?' Skye asked.

Charlie nodded, but her throat closed over as her father and Skye took her down the hospital corridor, and she had to breathe in deeply through her nose in an attempt to stay calm.

The baby was in a Humidicrib in a special isolation ward and they could only look at her through a glass window.

Isla was naked except for a disposable nappy, and she was lying on her side with her wrinkled hands folded together and tucked under her little chin. A tube had been inserted into her nose and was taped across her cheek to hold it in place. Monitor wires were taped to her tummy and her feet. Such a sad and scary sight.

'Oh, poor darling.' The cry burst from Charlie. She couldn't help it. Her heart was breaking.

She tried to imagine a doctor operating on such a tiny wee thing. Thank heavens she had found the money for the very best surgeon possible. She suppressed a nervous shiver. This was hardly the time to dwell on the details of what earning that money entailed. Her baby sister was her focus.

As she watched, Isla gave a little stretch. One hand opened, tiny fingers fluttering, bumping herself on the chin so that she frowned, making deep furrows across her forehead. Now she looked like a little old lady.

'Oh,' Charlie cried again. 'She's so sweet. She's gorgeous.'

She turned to her father and Skye, who were

holding hands and gazing almost fearfully at their daughter.

'I've found a way to raise the money,' Charlie told them quickly.

Skye gasped. 'Not enough to take her to Boston, surely?'

'Yes.'

Skye gave a dazed shake of her head. 'With a special nurse to accompany her?'

'Yes, there's money to cover all those costs.'

'Oh, my God.'

Skye went white and clutched at her husband's arm, looking as if she might faint.

'Are you sure about this, Charlie?' her father demanded tensely. 'I don't want Skye to get her hopes up and then be disappointed.'

Charlie nodded. 'I have the cheque in my handbag.' Nervously, she drew out the slim, astonishing slip of paper. 'It might take a few days before the money's deposited into your bank account, but it's a proper bank cheque. It's all above board.'

'Good heavens.' Her father stared at the cheque and then stared at his daughter in disbelief. 'How on earth did you manage this? What's this House of St Romain? Some kind of church group? Who could be so generous?'

This was the awkward bit. Charlie had no intention of telling her dad and Skye about Rafe and the fact that she'd agreed to be a stand-in as a European prince's pretend fiancée. For starters, they wouldn't believe her—they would think she'd taken drugs, or had been hit on the head and was hallucinating.

But also, telling them about Rafe would involve telling them about Olivia, and this wasn't the right moment to bring up that particular can of worms. Charlie was angry about her father's silence over such an important matter as her sister. On the way to the hospital she'd allowed herself a little weep about her absent mother and unknown twin sister, but she'd consoled herself that by accepting the role of fake fiancée she was actually taking a step closer to finding the truth.

For now, though, they had to stay focused on Isla.

'Dad, you have my word this money is from a legitimate source and there's nothing to worry about. But it's complicated, I'll admit that. You'll have to trust me for now. You've got enough to worry about with Isla. Let me take care of the money side of things.'

'I hope you haven't gone into debt, Charlie. You know I won't be able to pay this back.'

'You don't have to worry about that either. The only issue will be finding someone to run the gallery while I'm—' Charlie quickly changed tack. 'I'll be—busy organising everything. Do you think Amy Thornton might be available?'

'I'm pretty sure Amy's free. But for heaven's sake, Charlie—' For a long moment her father stared at her. 'If you don't want to tell me, I'm not going to press you,' he said finally. 'I do trust you, darling. I know you won't be breaking any laws.'

'Of course not. I've managed to find a generous—' Charlie swallowed. 'A generous benefactor, who wishes to remain anonymous.'

'How amazing. That's—that's wonderful.'

Charlie forced a bright smile. 'So now your job is to get busy with talking to doctors and airlines and everything that's involved with getting Isla well.'

'I don't know what to say.' Tears glistened in her father's eyes. 'Thank you, Charlie.' His voice was ragged and rough with emotion. 'Not every girl would be so caring about a half-sister.'

The three of them hugged, and Skye was weeping, but to Charlie's relief her father quickly broke away to find a nursing sister. In no time he and the nurse were making the necessary arrangements. Her dad was stepping up to the mark and adopting full responsibility.

She was free to go.

She'd never realised how scary that could be.

A frenetic hour later Charlie had rung Amy Thornton and secured her services at the gallery for the next month. She'd showered, changed into jeans and a sweater for the long flight, and had taken her cat, Dolly, next door to be minded by Edna, a kind and very accommodating elderly neighbour.

As she frantically packed, she couldn't believe she was actually doing this. She didn't dare to stop and think too hard about her sudden whirlwind decision—she knew she'd have second, third and fourth thoughts about the craziness of it all. The only safe way to keep her swirling emotions under control was to keep busy.

Finally, she was packed and ready with her passport, which was, fortunately, up to date.

Rafe arrived just as Charlie was sitting on her suitcase trying to get it closed. He shot a curious and approving glance around her tiny flat with its bright red walls and black and white furnishings, which she was quietly rather proud of, and which normally included her rather beautiful black and white cat.

Then he eyed her bulging luggage and frowned.

'I know it's winter in Montaigne,' Charlie offered as her excuse. 'So I threw in every warm thing I have. But I'm not sure that any of my stuff is really suitable for snowy weather.'

Or for an aspiring princess, she added silently.

Rafe passed this off with a shrug. 'You can always buy new warm clothes when you get there.'

Yes, she could do that if she hadn't already reallocated his generous payment. She felt a tad guilty as she snapped the locks on her suitcase shut.

Rafe picked it up. 'I have a taxi waiting.'

'Right.' Charlie stifled a nervous ripple. This was going to work out. And it wasn't a completely foolish thing to do. It was worthwhile. Really, it was. She would provide a front for Rafe while he got things sorted with Olivia and saved his country from some kind of economic ruin. And little Isla was getting a very important chance to have a healthy life.

Straightening her shoulders, she pinned on a brave smile. 'Let's get this show on the road,' she told Rafe.

To her surprise, he didn't immediately turn to head for the door. He took a step forward, leaned in and kissed her on both cheeks. She caught a whiff of expensive aftershave, felt the warm brush of his lips on her skin.

'Thank you for doing this, Charlie.' His eyes blazed with surprising emotion and warmth. 'It means a lot to me.'

Charlie wasn't sure what to say. When people did unexpectedly nice things she had a bad habit of crying. But she couldn't allow herself to cry now, so she nodded brusquely. Then she followed him out, shut the door, and slipped the key under the mat outside Edna's door, as they'd arranged.

As she did so, Edna's door opened to reveal the old lady with Dolly in her arms.

'We thought we'd wave you off,' Edna said, beaming a jolly smile as she lifted one of Dolly's white paws and waggled it. But then Edna saw Rafe and she forgot to wave or to smile. Instead she stood there, like a statue, eyes agog.

Great.

Charlie suppressed a groan. When she'd told her neighbour about her hastily arranged flight, she hadn't mentioned a male companion. Now *everyone* in their block of flats would know that Charlie Morisset had taken off on reckless impulse with a tall, dark and extremely handsome stranger.

Conversation was limited as the taxi whizzed across Sydney, although Rafe did comment on the beauty of the harbour and the magnificent

Opera House. In no time, they arrived at a private airport terminal that Charlie hadn't even known existed.

There was no queue, no waiting, no taking her shoes off for Security, not even tickets to be checked. Her passport was carefully examined though, by a round little Customs man with a moustache, who did a lot of bowing and scraping and calling Rafe 'Your Highness'. Then their luggage was trundled away and there was no more to do.

Rafe's plane was ready and waiting.

Oh, boy. Charlie had been expecting a smallish aircraft that would probably need to make many stops between Australia and Europe. This plane was enormous.

'Do you own this?' she couldn't help asking Rafe.

He chuckled. 'I don't need to *own* a jet. They're very easy to charter, and I have a priority listing.'

'I'm sure you do,' she muttered under her breath.

At that point, she might have felt very nervous about flying off into the unknown with a man she'd only just met, but Rafe took her arm as they crossed the tarmac, tucking it companionably under his, and somehow everything felt a little better and safer. And he kept a firm steadying hand at her elbow as they mounted the steps and entered the plane.

Then Charlie forgot to be nervous. She was too busy being impressed. And overawed.

The interior of Rafe's chartered jet was like no other plane she'd ever seen or imagined. It was more like a hotel suite—with padded armchairs and sofas, and a beautiful dining table.

Everything was exquisite, glamorous and tasteful, decorated in restful blues and golds. As they went deeper into the plane, there were wonderful double beds—two of them, Charlie was relieved to see—complete with banks of pillows, soft wall lamps, and beautiful gold quilts.

The only things to remind her that this was a jet were the narrowness of the space and the lines of porthole windows down each side.

'OK,' she said, sending Rafe a bright grin. 'I'm impressed.'

'I hope you have a comfortable flight.'

'There'd have to be something wrong with me if I didn't.'

He looked amused as he smiled. 'Come and take a seat ready for take-off.'

Rafe's bodyguards had boarded the plane as well, but they disappeared into a section behind closed doors, leaving Rafe and Charlie in total privacy as they strapped themselves into stupendously luxurious white leather chairs. An excessively polite, young female flight attendant appeared, dressed demurely in powder blue and carrying a tray with glasses of champagne, complete with strawberries and a platter with cheese and grapes and nuts.

Oh, my. Until now, Charlie had been too busy and preoccupied to give much thought to what being a prince's fiancée involved, but it seemed this gig might be a ton of fun. Despite her worries about Isla and about all the unknowns that lay ahead of her, she should try to relax and enjoy it.

The flight was a breeze. First there was a scrumptious meal of roasted leek soup, followed by slow-cooked lamb and a tiny mousse made from white chocolate and cherries, and to drink there was wonderful French champagne.

Charlie gave Rafe a blissful smile as she patted her lips with the napkin. 'This is so delicious,' she said, for perhaps the third or fourth time.

He looked slightly bemused and she wondered if she'd gone a bit too far with her praise.

Of course, she'd been out with guys who'd fed her beautiful meals before this, but it was still an experience she could never get tired of. At home, she'd done most of the cooking before her father's marriage, and she now cooked for herself in the flat, but she'd never seemed to have time to learn more than the basics. Fancy gourmet food was a treat.

After dinner, Rafe said he had business to attend to and was soon busy frowning at his laptop. Charlie, yawning and replete, changed into pyjamas and climbed into an incredibly comfortable bed.

She expected to lie awake for ages mulling over the amazing and slightly scary turn her life had taken in one short day, but with a full tummy, an awesomely comfy bed, and the pleasant, deep, throbbing drone of the plane's engines, she fell asleep quickly.

Rafe suppressed a sigh as he watched Charlie fall asleep with almost childlike speed. Was that the sleep of innocence? He hadn't slept well for weeks—since the night of his father's death. There always seemed to be too much to worry about. First his guilt and despair that he'd been so caught up in his good-time life that he'd missed any chance to bid his father farewell. And then the weighty realities of assuming his sudden new responsibilities.

Now he scanned the emails he'd downloaded before boarding the plane, but there was still no good news about Olivia, or about the intelligence surveillance on Claude Pontier.

Rafe was confident that it wouldn't be long now, before they caught Pontier out. Montaigne's Head of Police, Chief Dameron, was a wise, grey-haired fellow, approaching retirement, so he had a wealth of experience. He'd come up through the ranks, earning his promotions through hard work and diligence, but he'd also been trained by the FBI.

Consequently, his combination of old-school police procedures with the latest technical surveillance savvy was invaluable. Rafe had every faith in him.

Now Rafe looked again towards the bed where Charlie slept, curled on her side with golden curls tumbling on the pillow, and he was surprised by the tenderness he felt towards this girl who'd so readily stepped into her sister's shoes. He wondered if their similarities were more than skin deep.

He suspected that the two girls' personalities were quite different, found himself hoping for this, in fact. And that made no sense at all.

When Charlie woke, the flight attendant was offering her a tray with orange juice and a pot of coffee.

'We'll be landing in Dubai in less than an hour,' she was told.

Really?

A glance through the doorway showed Rafe, already up and dressed and sitting on one of the lounges, working on his computer again. Or perhaps he'd been working all night? Charlie downed her orange juice and hurried to her private bathroom to change out of her pyjamas and wash her face.

She took her tray with the coffee through to the lounge.

'Good morning.' Once again, Rafe's smile held a hint of amusement. 'You slept well?'

'Unbelievably well,' Charlie agreed.

She settled into a lounge and took a sip of coffee. 'I didn't realise we'd be landing in Dubai. I guess we need to refuel?'

'It's not a long stop,' he said. 'But yes, we need to refuel and my good friend, Sheikh Faysal Daood Taariq, wants to give us breakfast.'

'Did you say a—a sheikh?'

'That's right.'

Charlie stared at Rafe in dismay. The thought of breakfast with a sheikh was even more confronting than stepping onto a private jet with a prince. She took a deeper sip of her coffee, as if it might somehow clear her head. 'Are you sure I should come to this breakfast?'

'Well, yes, of course,' said Rafe. 'You're my fiancée.'

'Oh, yes.' This demanded more coffee. 'Yes,

of course.' Charlie's hand shook ever so slightly as she refilled her cup from the silver pot. The deeper ramifications of becoming her sister Olivia were only just sinking in.

This, now, was her reality check. When she stepped off this plane, she would no longer be Charlie Morisset.

'You'll like Faysal,' Rafe told her with a reassuring smile. 'I've known him for years. We met when we were both at Oxford.'

'I—I see. And he's a proper sheikh, but you just call him Faysal?'

'Yes, and you can call him Faysal, too. He's very relaxed and used to westerners.'

'But will I need to wear a headscarf, or curtsy or anything?'

Rafe grinned. 'Not today. Not in his home.'

'What about shaking hands? Is that OK?'

'Offering your hand would be perfectly acceptable. You'll find Faysal is a charming gentleman.'

'Right.' Charlie looked down at her hands and realised she should probably have painted her nails. She looked at her simple T-shirt and trousers. 'I should probably change into something a bit dressier.'

'Not at all. You'll be fine, Charlie. Relax.' Rafe closed his laptop and slipped it into an overhead locker. 'It's time to strap ourselves back into the seat belts for landing.'

The flight attendant collected their coffee trays, and, once they were belted, she disappeared as the plane began its descent.

In her seat beside Rafe, Charlie couldn't resist asking more questions. 'So, this Faysal—how many wives does he have?'

This brought another chuckle. 'None at all so far. He's still enjoying the life of a bachelor.'

'Right. So he's a playboy?'

'Of course,' Rafe said with a knowing smile.

And I suppose you were a playboy, too, before your father died.

This sudden realisation bothered Charlie more than it should have. Why should she care about Rafe's sex life? It was none of her business—although it did make her wonder again about why Olivia had run away from him.

'And for your information, Faysal's father only has *four* wives,' Rafe said.

'Oh?' she replied airily. 'Only four?'

Rafe shrugged. 'It's a sign of the times. His grandfather had forty.'

Good grief.

After only a very short time in Dubai, Charlie realised how truly ignorant she was about this part of the world. Of course, she'd expected to see regal and haughty, dark-bearded men in flowing white robes, and she knew these men were extraordinarily wealthy and heavily into horse-racing and speed-cars and living the high life. But she hadn't been prepared for the over-the-top opulence.

On the short journey from the airport to Sheikh Faysal Daood Taariq's home, she saw a car painted in gold—and yes, Rafe assured her, it was *real* gold—and another studded with diamonds. And good grief, there was even, in one bright red sports car, a leopard!

A proper live, wild creature. Massive, with a glorious coat of spots and a silver lead around its neck. The leopard was sitting in a front passenger seat beside a handsome young man in white robes and dark sunglasses.

Gobsmacked, Charlie turned to Rafe. 'That wasn't really a leopard, was it?'

He grinned. 'It was indeed.'

'But it couldn't be. How can they?'

Rafe shrugged. 'Welcome to Dubai. Extravagance abounds here and dreadfully expensive exotic pets are all the rage.'

'But surely—' Charlie wanted to protest about the dangers. About animal rights, but she stopped herself just in time.

'Listen, Charlie.' They were in the back seat of a huge limousine and Rafe leaned a little closer, speaking quietly. 'Try not to be too surprised by anything you see here.' He waved his hand to the view beyond the car's window, as they passed a grand palace at the end of an avenue lined on both sides with fountains and palm trees.

'I can't help being amazed,' she said somewhat meekly. But she knew she had to try harder. 'I guess Olivia's used to all this,' she said. 'Her jaw wouldn't be dropping every five minutes.'

Rafe nodded. 'Exactly.'

In that moment, Charlie realised something else. 'You've brought me here to your friend's house as a test, haven't you? It's a kind of trial run for me?'

Rafe's only answer was a smile, but Charlie knew she was right. Visiting his good friend, Faysal, was a kind of fast-track apprenticeship for her in her new role as Rafe's fiancée. If she made any gross mistakes here, the errors would remain 'in house' so to speak.

But she wasn't going to make mistakes. She could do this. In Sheikh Faysal's home, she would ensure that she had perfect posture and perfect manners. She would remember to stand straight, sit with her knees together, and never cross her legs, always be polite and eat neatly, and—

And it would be exhausting to be a full-time princess.

But Charlie was determined to pass any test Rafe St Romain presented. Of course, she could hold her tongue and play the role she'd been assigned. After all, he was paying her *very* handsomely.

Now, with her thoughts sorted, she realised that their car was turning. Huge iron gates were rolling open to allow them entry to a gravelled drive and a tall, white, three-storeyed house decorated with arches.

The car stopped at a heavily embossed front door, which opened immediately to reveal a dark-haired, olive-skinned man almost as handsome as Rafe.

'Rafe and Olivia!' he cried, throwing wide his arms. 'How lovely to see you both again. Welcome!'

Breakfast at Faysal's was wonderful, as always, and to Rafe's relief Charlie behaved admirably.

They dined on the terrace beside the swimming pool, where they were served Arabic coffee made from coffee beans ground with cardamom and saffron, as well as spicy chick peas and *balabet*, a dish of sweetened vermicelli mixed with eggs and spices. There were also delicious pancakes flavoured with cardamom and coloured with saffron and served with date syrup.

Charlie was on her best behaviour, and Rafe knew she was trying hard not to be too overly impressed by everything she saw and tasted. But he could also tell that she was enjoying the meal immensely, possibly even more than she'd enjoyed last evening's meal on the plane.

Just the same, she managed not to gush over the food, and she only jumped once when Faysal called her Olivia.

She couldn't quite hide her fascination with her surroundings, though. Her bright blue eyes widened with obvious delight at the fountains and the terraced gardens and the arcade decorated with exquisite blue and gold tiled mosaics. And Rafe thought she was just a little too impressed by Faysal, who was, as always, handsome and ultra-charming.

Nevertheless, the meeting went rather well, and Rafe was feeling relaxed when Charlie retired to the powder room.

As soon as she'd left, however, Faysal, who had dressed today in European trousers and a white polo shirt instead of his customary white robes, looked across the table to Rafe with a narrowed and sceptical dark gaze.

'So,' he said, his lips tilting with amusement. 'Who the hell is that girl, Rafe?'

Inwardly groaning, Rafe feigned ignorance. 'You know who she is. She's my fiancée, Olivia. What game are you playing?'

'That's the very same question I want to ask you. You're trying to pull a swift one over me, old boy.' Faysal nodded to the corridor where Charlie had disappeared. 'That girl is Olivia's double, I'll grant you that, but, unless she's had a complete personality transplant, she is not the girl I met in Saint-Tropez and again at your engagement ball.'

Rafe sighed heavily as he remembered the extravagant ball he'd hosted. At the time he'd needed to make a big stir about his engagement and to show Chancellor Pontier how serious he was. He hoped there hadn't been too many guests as astute as Faysal. 'Is it really that obvious?'

Faysal's smile was sympathetic as he nodded. 'I'll admit I observe women with a deeper interest than most.'

This was true, but still Rafe was afraid he had a problem.

'Her name's Charlie,' he said. 'Or rather,

Charlotte. She's Olivia's twin sister. I tracked her down in Australia.'

'Australia? So that was the accent.'

Rafe grimaced. 'Is that what gave her away? Her accent?'

'Not really.' Faysal eyed Rafe with a level and serious gaze.

'What, then?' Rafe demanded impatiently.

'Her sincerity.'

Hell.

Rafe knew exactly what Faysal meant. There was a genuineness about Charlie that had been totally absent in her sister. He gave a helpless shrug. 'I can't do much about that.'

'No,' Faysal observed quietly. Then he frowned. 'So what happened to Olivia? She hasn't been abducted, has she?'

'No, I wouldn't be sitting here passing the time of day with you if that was the case.' Rafe shrugged. 'She ran away.'

Faysal looked only mildly surprised. 'She panicked, in other words.'

'Yes, I think she must have.'

His friend gave a slow, thoughtful nod. 'Getting engaged to that girl wasn't your smartest move, my friend.'

'I know.' Rafe sighed again. 'As you know, it was all about convenience. It was such a shock when my father died. So unexpected.'

'The pressures of being an only child,' Faysal mused. 'If your mother had still been alive…'

Faysal didn't finish the sentence, but Rafe knew exactly what he was implying. His mother had died three years ago, but if she'd still been alive she would have seen through Olivia Belaire in a heartbeat. And in no time at all, his mother would have produced a list of a dozen or more highly suitable young women for him to choose from.

These girls would have been from good schools and families. They would probably have all had university degrees and perfect deportment and grooming and impeccable manners and be interested in good works. The list of his mother's requirements for a princess were numerous. She had never approved of the girls Rafe had dated.

His criteria for selecting a female companion had been quite different from his mother's. But those carefree days were over.

'If you can see through Charlie,' he said, somewhat dispiritedly, 'I've got a problem on my hands, haven't I?'

His friend shook his head and smiled. 'No, not a problem, Rafe. If you play your cards correctly, I'd say your Charlie could be quite an asset.'

No, Rafe thought, *Faysal's reading this wrong.*

His friend might have approved of Charlie's prettiness and sincerity, but he hadn't seen her horror at the thought of actually having to marry him.

'She's a temporary stopgap,' he said firmly. 'That's all.'

CHAPTER FIVE

'SO, ARE YOU going to give me a performance appraisal?'

Charlie and Rafe were back in the plane and taking off for Europe when she posed this question.

She'd tried her hardest to be cool and sophisticated in Faysal's home and she needed to know if her efforts had been satisfactory. After all, there wasn't much time to lift her act before they arrived in Montaigne.

She was watching Rafe intently, waiting for his answer, and she didn't miss his frown, although he very quickly hid it behind a smooth smile.

'You were perfect,' he said.

'Are you sure?' She'd tried really hard to lose her accent, but she suspected that he wasn't being totally honest. 'I need to hear the truth, Rafe. I don't want to let you down.'

Which was a noble way of saying that she

didn't want to face the embarrassment of being caught out.

'You were fine,' he said with a hint of impatience.

Charlie wasn't sure that 'fine' was good enough, but she didn't want to pester him and become annoying. She consoled herself that Rafe would have told her if she'd made a major blunder.

'So there's nothing you need to warn me about before I arrive in your country?' she tried one more time.

Rafe smiled. 'No, just be yourself, Charlie. It would be different if you really were my fiancée, but for now, I think you'll do well just as you are.'

'Right.' Charlie wished the mention of Rafe's 'real' fiancée didn't bother her so much.

'Just try to look as if you're enjoying yourself,' he said.

She couldn't help smiling. 'That shouldn't be too hard.'

It was true. Everything about this trip so far had been wonderfully exciting. If Charlie hadn't been so worried about poor little Isla, she would have looked on this as the adventure of a lifetime.

As soon as they reached their cruising height, Rafe opened his laptop again. Apparently, he was studying everything he could about mining, so that he could outwit the Leroy Mining Company who wanted to wreck his Alps.

For most of the flight Charlie watched movies. Her head still buzzed with a host of questions—questions about Rafe, about his family and his country, and what he expected of her—but he was clearly preoccupied. And, as he'd made it quite clear, she didn't have the responsibility of a 'real' job.

That belonged to Olivia.

Her sister.

Charlie felt a deep pang at the thought of the girl who was her mirror image. *Her sister.* They shared the same mother. Had shared the same *womb.* The same DNA.

How could her father have kept this secret from her? Learning about it now, Charlie felt hurt. Deeply hurt, as if she'd been denied something precious. The other half of herself.

She wondered how on earth the decision had been made. Obviously her parents had decided to split and take a child each. But how had they made that choice?

Tossed a coin? Drawn straws?

Charlie wouldn't dwell on the fact that her mother had rejected her and chosen Olivia. It could warp her mind if she let that sink in too deeply. The important thing to remember was that she loved her father very much. She'd had a wonderful childhood and they'd shared many adventures, and they had a great relationship. She couldn't imagine her life without her sweet, dreamy dad.

But she also couldn't deny that her feelings about Olivia were incredibly complicated. On one level she longed to meet her sister and get to know her, but on another level she was stupidly jealous that Olivia was going to marry this deadly handsome Prince.

When Rafe found her.

They arrived in Grenoble mid-afternoon, descending through thick clouds into a world of whiteness. Snow blanketed every rooftop and field and Charlie was so excited she could hardly drag herself from the window when the flight attendant delivered her coat and scarf.

'Do you have boots?' Rafe asked, eyeing Charlie's flimsy shoes. 'You might need them.'

'They're packed away in my suitcase.'

'Hmm.' He came closer and fingered the fabric of her coat.

Charlie could tell by his frown that the coat was inadequate.

'This should be OK to get you from here to my car,' he said. 'But you'll have to get something thicker and warmer for Montaigne.'

'Yes, I dare say.' The new coat would probably need to be a good deal more glamorous, too, Charlie thought, as she noted the elegant cut of Rafe's thick overcoat. In other words, she would have to spend a big chunk of her meagre savings on a coat that she'd only need for a couple of weeks. But she couldn't bring herself to ask Rafe for more money.

Despite Rafe's warning, Charlie wasn't prepared for the blast of frigid air that hit her as she stepped out of the plane. The cold seemed to bite straight through her coat and penetrate to her very bones.

'Are you OK?' Rafe asked, slipping an arm around her shoulders. 'Charlie, you're shivering. Here, take my coat.'

'No, it's all right. We're almost there.'

Welcome warmth enveloped them as they left the tarmac and the airport's doors slid open for them. But now there was something else to worry about.

'Are there likely to be paparazzi here?' she asked.

Rafe slanted her a smile. 'There shouldn't be. I've tried to keep my movements undercover.'

Just the same, Charlie turned up the collar on her coat and tried to look relaxed when heads turned their way. She kept a fixed little smile in place as she walked with Rafe to the chauffeur waiting with a sleek black, unmarked car. All was well. So far.

Grenoble lay at the very foot of the Alps, so it wasn't long before the car was climbing the mountainous slopes. Snowflakes drifted all around them, and Charlie watched through the car windows in delight.

'It doesn't snow in Sydney,' she told Rafe. 'I've seen snow in the Blue Mountains and on the tops of the peaks in Nepal, but we were there in summer. I've never seen it like this. With snow simply *everywhere*.'

It was only then that she caught Rafe's warning frown and his quick glance to the chauffeur sitting just in front of him.

Oh, help.

Charlie flinched. What an idiot she was. Of course, this chauffeur would talk to the rest of Rafe's staff about the strange change in their master's fiancée. Damn. She'd only just arrived and already she'd made a huge blunder.

Her face was burning as she pressed her lips tightly together. She was such a fool. Turning away sharply, she held her eyes wide open to try to hold back any hint of tears.

Until now, she hadn't doubted that she could do this, but with this first silly gaffe the enormity of her task almost overwhelmed her. There would be so many chances to make mistakes—with servants, with government officials, with Rafe's friends, shopkeepers…

Rafe reached for her hand and she jumped, but his touch was gentle.

'Don't worry,' he murmured, giving her hand an encouraging squeeze.

'But—' Charlie nodded meaningfully towards the back of the chauffeur's head.

'It's OK,' Rafe said quietly, still holding her hand. 'I'll speak to him.' After a bit, he added, 'You'll probably prefer not to have a personal maid.'

Heavens no. Charlie supposed Olivia might have had a maid, but she was bound to make way too many slip-ups under that level of vigilant attention. 'I don't think a maid will be necessary,' she said carefully.

Rafe nodded.

Deeply grateful, Charlie managed a weak smile. 'I'll get the hang of this,' she promised.

'Of course you will.'

His hand was warm on hers.

Already, she was beginning to like Rafe. Too much.

The early twilight was growing darker by the minute. Below them, the lights of Grenoble twinkled prettily, and as the road wound ever upwards, night pressed in. They passed clusters of steep-roofed chalets that glowed with welcoming warmth, but for most of the journey the Alps loomed dark and slightly ominous, the car's headlights catching huge rocky outcrops topped with snow.

Charlie wondered how long it would take to reach Montaigne, but she refrained from asking Rafe and once again exposing her ignorance. It wasn't easy for a natural chatterbox to remain silent, but discretion was her new watchword.

From time to time, Rafe talked to her about matters that he needed to attend to over the next few days. Meetings, luncheons, more meetings, dinners.

'You'll be busy,' Charlie said, and she wondered what she would do while Rafe was buzzing around attending to his princely duties.

'You'll probably need to attend some of these functions,' he said. 'Especially the dinners, but I'll try to keep your duties light. You'll have plenty of time for shopping.'

Shopping. *Oh, dear.*

It was about an hour and a half later that they reached Montaigne perched high in an Alpine valley. The capital city was incredibly pretty, bathed in the clear moonlight, with lights shining from a thousand windows. The valley looked like a bowl of sparkling, golden flakes.

'Home,' said Rafe simply.

'It's very beautiful,' Charlie told him.

He nodded and smiled. 'You must be so tired. It's been a long journey.'

They were pulling up at the front steps of a fairy-tale castle. Charlie forgot her tiredness. She was far too excited.

'*Bonsoir,* Your Highness. *Bonsoir, mademoiselle.*'

A dignified fellow in a top hat and a braided greatcoat opened the car door for them. Another man collected their luggage.

Rafe ushered Charlie up a short flight of snow-spotted steps and through the huge open front doors. A woman aged around fifty and dressed in a neat navy-blue skirt and jacket greeted them with a smile.

'Good evening, Chloe.' Rafe addressed her quickly in French, as she greeted them and took their coats. 'Mademoiselle Olivia is very tired, so we'll retire early this evening, but we'd like some coffee and perhaps a little soup?'

'Yes, I'll have it sent up straight away, Your Highness.'

'That would be very good, thank you.'

Charlie managed with difficulty to refrain from staring about her like an awestruck Aussie tourist, but Rafe's castle was amazingly beautiful. There were white marble floors and enormous flower arrangements, huge gold-framed mirrors, chandeliers, and a grand marble staircase carpeted in deep royal blue.

Despite her nervousness, she planned to drink in every moment that she spent here, and one day she would tell her grandchildren about it. But she wasn't sure she could ever get used to hearing Rafe addressed as 'Your Highness'. Thank heavens she was only *mademoiselle.*

'I'll show you to your room,' Rafe told her.

To her surprise, they didn't proceed up the staircase. A lift had been fitted into the castle.

'My grandfather had this lift installed for my grandmother,' Rafe told her. 'Grandmère had a problem with her knees as she got older.'

'It must make life a lot easier for everyone else, too,' said Charlie.

'Yes. Here we are on the second floor. Your room is on the right.'

Charlie's room was, in fact, an entire suite, with a huge bedroom, bathroom and sitting room. And although the castle seemed to be heated, there was even a fireplace, where flames burned a bright welcome, and off the bedroom a small study, complete with a desk, a telephone and an assortment of stationery ready for her use.

The whole area was carpeted in a pretty rose

pink with cream and silver accessories, and there were at least three bowls of pink roses. Charlie's suitcase had already been placed at the foot of the bed and it looked rather shabby and out of place.

'This is rather old-fashioned compared with your flat in Sydney,' Rafe said.

'But it's gorgeous,' protested Charlie, who couldn't believe he would even *try* to make a comparison. 'Oh, and look at the view!' She hurried over to the high, arched window set deep in the stone wall with a sill wide enough for sitting and dreaming.

Below, the lights of Montaigne glowed warm and bright in the snowy setting.

'I can't believe this.' She was grinning as she turned back to Rafe. 'It's so incredibly picture perfect.'

'There's a remote control here beside the bed.' Rafe picked it up and demonstrated. 'It makes the glass opaque for when you want to sleep.'

'How amazing.' Charlie watched in awe as the glass grew dark and then, at another flick of the switch, became clear again. 'It's magic. Like being in a fairy tale. Aren't you lucky to actually live here?'

His smile was careful. 'Even fairy tales have their dark and dangerous moments.'

'Well, yes, I guess.' Charlie wasn't sure if

he was joking or serious. 'I suppose there are always wicked witches and wolves and evil spells.' And in Rafe's case, a wicked Chancellor and evil miners who wanted to wreck his country. 'But at least fairy tales give you a happy ending.'

'Unless you're the wolf,' suggested Rafe.

Charlie frowned at him. 'You're very pessimistic all of a sudden.'

'I am. You're right. I apologise.' But Rafe still looked sad as he stood there watching her.

Charlie wondered if he was thinking about his father who had died so recently. Or perhaps he was thinking about Olivia, wishing his real fiancée were here in his castle, preparing for their marriage. Instead he was left with an improvised substitute who would soon leave again.

Or were there other things worrying him? He'd mentioned the mining threat, but he probably had a great many other issues to deal with. Affairs of state.

She was pondering this when he smiled suddenly. 'I must say I'm not surprised that you believe in happy endings, Charlie.'

She thought instantly of Isla. 'It's terribly important to think positively. Why not believe? It's better than giving up.'

He dismissed this with a shrug. 'But it's a bit like asking me if I believe in fairies. Happy endings are all very well in theory, but I find that real life is mostly about compromise.'

Compromise?

Charlie stared at him in dismay. She'd never liked the idea of compromise. It seemed like such a cop-out. She never wanted to give up on important hopes and dreams and to settle for second best.

She wanted to protest, to set Rafe straight, but there was something very earnest in his expression that silenced her.

She thought about his current situation. He'd been forced to arrange a hasty, convenient marriage to save his country, instead of waiting till he found the woman he loved. That was certainly a huge compromise for both Rafe and for Olivia.

When Rafe looked ahead to the future, he could probably foresee many times when he would be required to set aside his own needs and desires and to put duty to his country first.

It was a chastening thought. Charlie supposed she'd been pretty foolish to come sailing in here, all starry-eyed, and immediately suggest that living in a castle was an automatic ticket to a fairy-tale life. She was about to apologise when there was a knock at the door.

A young man had arrived with their supper.

'Thanks, Guillaume,' Rafe said as the fellow

set a tray on the low table in front of the fire. To Charlie, he said, 'I thought we'd be more comfortable eating in here tonight.' When Guillaume had left, he added, 'You don't mind if I join you?'

'No, of course not.' After all, it was what the servants would expect of an engaged couple.

They sat on sofas facing each other. The coffee smelled wonderful, as did the chicken soup, and the setting was incredibly cosy. Charlie looked at the flickering flames, the bowls of steaming soup and the crusty bread rolls.

The scene was almost homely, hardly like being in a royal castle at all, and for Charlie there was an extra sprinkle of enchantment, no doubt provided by the hunky man who, having shed his overcoat, looked relaxed again now in his jeans and dark green sweater.

Rafe's comments about compromise were sobering though, and no doubt they were the check she needed. Royals might not be dogged by the money worries that had plagued her for most of her life, but their money came with serious responsibilities.

Was that why Olivia ran away?

When they finished their soup, Rafe called for a nightcap, which was promptly delivered, and as he and Charlie sipped the rich, smooth cognac he watched the play of firelight on Charlie's curly hair, on her soft cheeks and lips. It was only with great difficulty that he managed to restrain himself from joining her on her sofa.

But man, he was tempted. There was a sweetness about Charlie that—

No, he wasn't going to make comparisons with her sister. He couldn't waste time or energy berating himself for the error of judgement that had landed him with Olivia Belaire. Regret served no useful purpose.

'Tomorrow, when you're ready, my secretary, Mathilde, will bring you a list of your engagements,' he said, steering his thoughts strictly towards business. 'Including your shopping and hair appointments.'

Charlie looked worried. 'But I won't have *appointments* for *shopping*, will I?'

'Yes. The stores find it helpful to plan ahead. They can make sure that the right staff is available to give you the very best assistance.'

'I see.' Charlie still looked worried. 'Will your secretary also give me a list of the sorts of clothes I need?'

'No, Monique at Belle Robe will look after that. If you show Monique your list of engagements, she'll be able to advise you on dresses, shoes, handbags or whatever.'

'I—I see.'

Was it his imagination, or had Charlie grown pale?

Why? Surely all women loved shopping? Her sister had enthusiastically embraced the shopping expeditions he'd paid for. Unfortunately, Olivia had also taken all those clothes with her when she left. They would have fitted Charlie perfectly.

'You'll have to try to enjoy the experience,' he said.

'Yes, of course. I'll try to behave like Olivia. I suppose she loved shopping.'

'Yes, she had quite a talent for it.'

Charlie lifted a thumbnail to her mouth as if she wanted to chew it. Then she must have realised her mistake and quickly dropped her hand to her lap with her fist tightly curled. 'So I need to be enthusiastic,' she said. 'I can do that.'

'And don't worry about the expense.'

To his dismay, Charlie looked more worried than ever. 'What's the matter, Charlie?'

She flashed him a quick, rather brave little smile. 'No problem, really. It's just that I'm so used to living on a budget and it's hard to throw off the habits of a lifetime.'

Rafe couldn't remember ever dating a girl who was cautious with money. This was a novel experience. 'These clothes won't have price tags,' he reassured her. 'So you needn't know the cost. And remember they're just costumes. They're your uniform, if you like, an important part of the job.'

'Of course.'

'And you don't have to worry about jewellery either,' he said next. 'There's a huge collection here in the castle vault. All my mother's and grandmother's things.'

'How—how lovely.'

'I imagine that sapphires and diamonds will suit you best.'

Charlie fingered one of her simple, pearl stud earrings, and Rafe suppressed yet another urge to join her on the couch, to trace the sweet pink curve of her earlobe, preferably with his lips. Then he would kiss her smooth neck—

He sat up straighter, cleared his throat. 'And you'll have a driver to take you everywhere.'

'Thank you.'

'Are you sure you wouldn't like a maid as well? A female companion?'

Charlie shook her head. 'If I had another girl hanging out with me, I'd be sure to chatter and give myself away.'

He smiled, knowing that this was true. Charlie was so honest and open, but he wished she weren't still looking so worried. He felt much better when she was smiling. He'd been growing rather used to her smiles.

He hoped his next suggestion wouldn't make her even more worried. 'I was hoping you might be able to visit a children's hospital,' he said carefully. 'It would be very helpful for your image.'

The change in Charlie was instantaneous. Her shoulders visibly relaxed and she uncrossed her legs and, yes, she actually smiled. 'Sure,' she said. 'I'd love that. I love kids. That's a great idea.'

The sudden reversal was puzzling until Rafe remembered that his men had reported Charlie visiting a hospital in Sydney just before she'd made her final decision to accompany him to Montaigne.

What was her interest in hospitals? He hadn't asked his men to follow up on this, but now he recalled the upsetting phone call from her father and wondered if that was the connection. He would have liked to question Charlie about it. But if she'd wanted to tell him, she would have done so by now, and there were limits to how far he could reasonably expect to pry into her private affairs.

After all, their relationship was strictly business.

Charlie yawned then, widely and noisily, and

Rafe was instantly on his feet. 'It's time I left you. You need to sleep.'

'I *am* pretty stuffed,' she admitted with a wan smile.

They both stood. Beside them, the fire glowed and danced.

'Goodnight, Charlie.'

'Goodnight, Rafe.'

Her eyes were incredibly blue, their expression curious, and he supposed she was wondering if he planned to kiss her.

He certainly wanted to kiss her. Wanted to rather desperately. He wanted to taste the sweetness of her soft lips. Wanted to kiss her slowly and comprehensively, right there, on the sofa, by the warmth of the fire. Wanted to feel the softness of her skin, feel the eagerness of her response. Rafe imagined that Charlie's uninhibited response would be rather splendid.

'I'll see you in the morning,' she said, eyeing him cautiously.

Rafe came to his senses. 'Yes.' He spoke brusquely, annoyed by his lapse. 'I usually have breakfast at seven-thirty, but you will be tired from the jet lag, so sleep as long as you wish. There's a phone by your bed, so just call for a maid when you wake. Have coffee, breakfast, whatever you want, brought here to your room. Take your time.'

'Thank you.'

Stepping forward, he kissed her politely on both cheeks. *'Bonne nuit,'* he said softly, and then turned and left her without looking back.

Don't do it, Rafe told himself as he walked away. *Don't mess with this girl. You know you'll only end up hurting her.*

Problem was, the habits Rafe had developed during his years of freedom were strong. He'd grown used to having almost any girl he fancied, usually without any strings attached.

Now he was surrounded by restrictions and almost every breath he took had a string attached. The press was watching him. Chancellor Pontier was watching him. For all he knew, the whole country was watching him. His enemies were waiting for him to stuff up, while his people were waiting for him to step up to the mark.

At times the weight of expectation and responsibility pressed so heavily Rafe could barely breathe. Even Charlie, despite her willingness to help him, was just another responsibility.

For her sake, he had to remember that.

Charlie checked her phone before she went to bed, but there was no message from her father.

She pressed the remote to darken the window and climbed into bed. The sheets were smooth and silky, they smelled of lavender and were trimmed with exquisite lace and embroidery. The pillow was soft but firm.

Nevertheless, she lay awake for ages, worrying about Isla. Did no news mean good news? Or was her father too busy to bother with texting? Were he and Skye and Isla already in the air on their way to Boston?

How was Isla?

She remembered the lecture she'd given Rafe about positive thinking. She should follow her own advice. She had to believe that all would be well. Isla's tiny heart would survive the long plane flight and the highly skilled doctors in Boston would make her well. The money Rafe had so generously handed over would be put to good use and this whole crazy venture would be worthwhile.

The money...

This was another thing for Charlie to worry about. How on earth could she afford the clothes she needed to carry off the role of Prince Rafael's fiancée? Why on earth hadn't she foreseen this problem?

Anxiously she tossed and turned, playing with the notion of coming clean, of telling Rafe about Isla and explaining what she'd done with his money. But there were problems with this revelation.

First, there was a chance that Rafe might not believe her and they could end up having a row about it. It was an unlikely outcome, Charlie admitted. Rafe appeared to be quite generous and reasonable.

But Charlie certainly didn't want to take advantage of his good nature. The thing was, she'd struck a deal with him and now she had to keep up her end of the bargain. To ask for more money on top of his ample payment would feel totally shabby.

Besides, if she tried to tell Rafe about her baby sister's condition and the impending surgery, she would almost certainly offload all her fears and then blubber all over him.

This was the last thing Prince Rafael of Montaigne needed. He hadn't brought her here to listen to her problems.

He had enough problems of his own.

Once she'd thought things through to this point, Charlie felt calmer. Lying in the darkness, she watched the flickering firelight and she thought about the lovely evening she and Rafe had spent together. She remembered the moment before he'd left when he stood there in the firelight, looking at her. So tall and dark and sexy, with an expression in his eyes that had set her heart thumping.

So intense he'd looked. For a giddy moment, she'd thought he was going to kiss her. Properly. Passionately. Her heart had carried on like a crazy thing, thrashing about like a landed fish.

Such a ridiculous reaction. Perhaps she could blame the jet lag. Tomorrow she'd feel much more like her old self.

CHAPTER SIX

When Charlie woke the next morning, she took a moment to get her bearings. She couldn't remember another time she'd ever woken to such sumptuous surroundings.

She reached for the remote and pressed the button, and—hey, presto! Bright sunlight streamed into her room.

She wondered how late she'd slept and snatched up her phone to check the time. It was nine o'clock, and there were four new messages on her phone.

Three messages were from her father. One told her that he and Skye and Isla were leaving for Boston. Another gave her their flight's departure and arrival times. A third message asked where she was.

Charlie didn't answer this specifically.

Have a safe flight, she wrote. Sending my love to you and to Skye and Isla. All's well here. C xxx.

She'd crossed so many time zones, she didn't even try to calculate where they might be by now. It was just good to know Isla was on her way and, at this point, all was well. Charlie sent up a prayer.

Keep Isla safe. Hang in there, sweetheart.

The last text message was from Rafe.

Good morning. I hope you've slept well. My secretary, Mathilde, would like to meet with you at eleven. Is this suitable?

Quickly she typed back that this would be fine.

Great, wrote Rafe. Any problems, give me a call.

Charlie wondered where he was. Then her tummy rumbled. She needed breakfast. Rather nervously, she lifted the phone beside the bed.

Immediately a woman's voice at the other end said, '*Bonjour*, Mademoiselle Olivia.'

'Oh,' said Charlie. '*Bonjour.*' In her best French she asked, 'Could I please have some coffee in my room?'

'Certainly, *mademoiselle*. Would you also like breakfast? An omelette perhaps?'

'An omelette would be lovely. *Merci.*'

'It will be with you very soon, Mademoiselle Olivia.'

'Thank you.'

This done, Charlie heaved a huge sigh of relief. Her first hurdle might have been a rather low bar in the scheme of things, but at least she'd cleared it without mishap.

A much higher hurdle came later, after the secretary Mathilde had given Charlie her engagement itinerary. She was expected to start clothes shopping this very day.

Not only did Charlie need a warmer overcoat, a new outfit was required for dinner this evening, another to wear for a daytime engagement the next day and a special gown for a gala event to be held in the castle in two evenings' time.

Charlie almost whimpered when she saw the list. She knew Rafe never dreamed that she would be paying for these clothes out of her own money, but she felt she had no other option. The problem was, her bank account wouldn't stretch to *four* expensive items of clothing, all fit for a princess. She would be lucky if she could afford one of these outfits, which meant she had no alternative but to get a cash advance on her credit card.

Ouch.

Shivering inside her inadequate coat, Charlie stepped out of the castle to find that fresh snow had fallen during the night. Now, in the early afternoon, it was clear and sunny, but the air was freezing. A chauffeur was waiting for her at the foot of the steps.

He was understandably surprised when Charlie asked him to take her to a bank before delivering her to Belle Robe, but he discreetly refrained from making any comment. Fortunately, the bank teller didn't seem to recognise her as the Prince's intended bride. Her cards were accepted without a hitch and she was able to withdraw a sickening amount of money.

Belle Robe was around the next corner.

Gulp.

Charlie had seen expensive clothing boutiques in Sydney, so she was used to store windows decorated with elegant mannequins dressed in glamorous gowns, but she'd never been inside one of these places before. Now she tried hard not to be overawed by the top-hatted doorman, the wide expanses of cream carpet, the gilt-framed floor-to-ceiling mirrors.

Madame Monique, who'd been assigned to attend to Charlie's needs, was pencil thin with cut-glass cheekbones and she was dressed in a severely straight black dress of fine wool. She also wore glasses with trendy black and white frames and her iron-grey hair was pulled tightly back into a low ponytail.

Another woman might have looked plain in such restrained attire but Monique managed to look incredibly elegant. No doubt her bright scarlet lipstick and nail polish helped.

Charlie supposed she should have painted her nails, too. She wondered if Olivia had always worn nail polish. It was another detail she should have checked with Rafe.

Monique was very organised and had a page set aside for Charlie in a thick gold-edged notebook. 'Welcome back again, Mademoiselle Olivia,' she said with a careful smile.

'Thank you,' said Charlie. 'How are you, Monique?'

Surprise flashed briefly in the woman's eyes, as if she hadn't expected this question. 'I'm very well, thank you, *mademoiselle*.' Her smile brightened. 'And now, His Highness has ordered quite a few more items for you, I believe.'

'Yes, I'm afraid so.'

Monique looked a little puzzled at this and Charlie winced. *Afraid so?* Had she really said that? What an idiot she was. She would have to behave far more confidently if she wanted to convince the people of Montaigne that she was Olivia Belaire. She was supposed to *adore* shopping.

She laughed quickly to try to cover her gaffe. 'So,' she said, brightly. 'I'm sure you have some wonderful suggestions.'

'Of course,' said Monique. 'I have a very

good idea what suits you now, so I've made a few selections to get us started.'

'Lovely,' Charlie enthused. 'I can't wait to try them on.'

They started with the coats and it was so hard to choose between a beautiful long red coat with a leather belt and another in black and white houndstooth. Eventually, with a little prompting from Monique, Charlie settled on the red.

For this evening's dinner, she chose a timelessly styled blue dress made from exquisitely fine wool. It was rather figure-hugging and designed to catch the eye, but Charlie supposed it was the sort of thing Rafe wanted her to wear. She tried not to blush when she saw her reflection in the mirror, but, heavens, she'd had no idea she could look so glamorous.

'Do you know what the daytime event for tomorrow will be?' asked Madame Monique, watching Charlie closely.

Charlie was relieved that she could answer this. 'I believe I'll be visiting the children's hospital.'

The woman's eyebrows rose, but she made no comment as she showed Charlie a rather demure dress in grey with a box neckline and a wide band around the waist.

'Hmm,' said Charlie. 'That's lovely, but do you have anything that's a bit more—fun?'

'Fun, Mademoiselle Olivia?' Madame Monique was clearly surprised.

Charlie wondered if she'd used the wrong French word. 'Something more appealing to the children, something a little more—relaxed?'

'Oh, I see, of course.' Monique went back to her racks, frowning.

Charlie followed her. The clothes were extremely elegant, but there were rather a lot of beiges and greys and blacks. She was wondering if she would be better off just wearing a pair of jeans and one of her own sweaters when something caught her eye.

'What about this?' she said, lifting out a hanger to inspect the dress more closely. It was a feminine shift dress with elbow-length sleeves and a delicate all-over print of little red sail boats with white sails on a navy-blue background. 'This would be perfect. Do you have it in my size?'

Now Monique looked worried. 'But, *mademoiselle*, don't you remember? You already have this dress. You bought it two weeks ago.'

'Oh.' Charlie wished she could sink through the floor. 'Yes, of course,' she said shakily. 'How silly of me. I—I took it home to Saint-Tropez, you see, when I—when I visited my mother—and I—'

It was awful to lie so blatantly and just saying the word 'mother' felt terribly wrong. She couldn't quite finish the sentence, but if Monique was baffled, and Charlie was sure that she had to be, she discreetly covered the reaction.

'What about this?' Monique lifted out a white dress with black polka dots and a short black jacket. 'I think this would suit you beautifully. And it certainly looks...*détendu*.'

This outfit did indeed suit Charlie very well and it had the right playful vibe she'd been hoping for. It was added to the stash, along with an *oh-my-God* evening gown of pale sea-green satin that was the most elegant and glamorous thing Charlie had ever clapped eyes on, let alone worn.

She felt a little faint as she wondered what the price tag might be.

'And now for your shoes,' said Monique.

The fainting sensation grew stronger for Charlie. *Oh, dear.* She had to sit down.

Monique fussed. 'Mademoiselle Olivia, are you all right? What can I get you? A glass of water perhaps? Coffee?'

'Perhaps some water,' said Charlie. 'Thank you.'

Monique tut-tutted when she returned with the water. 'Perhaps you are not well, *mademoiselle*.'

'No, I'm fine,' Charlie insisted, after taking several reviving sips. 'It's probably—' She was about to use jet lag as an excuse when she remembered that her sister, Olivia, hadn't been flying halfway across the world in a jet. 'I'm just a bit tired,' she said instead. 'And I was wondering—before we start on the shoes, would you mind telling me how much I have spent so far?'

This time, Madame Monique didn't try to cover her surprise. Her eyebrows shot high above her black and white spectacle frames. 'But you know there's no need to concern yourself, my dear. This goes on the St Romain account, does it not?'

Charlie had no idea what arrangement Rafe had made with Olivia. All she knew was that he'd paid her, Charlie, an extremely generous sum and she wouldn't dream of asking him for anything more.

'I'm paying for today's purchases,' she said, but as the words left her mouth she saw Monique's expression of jaw-dropping shock and knew that she'd made yet another mistake.

The dinner that evening was an official affair with some of Montaigne's most important businessmen and their wives. Charlie wore the blue wool dress and a new pair of skin-toned high heels that she hoped would go with almost everything, although Madame Monique had persuaded her that she needed black boots to go with her overcoat.

'You look beautiful,' Prince Rafael told her when he saw her.

'Thanks.' It was the first time that day that Charlie had seen him and, to her dismay, just watching him walk into the drawing room in a dark suit and tie caused a jolt to her senses. To make matters worse, he reached for her hand.

Ridiculous tingles shot over her skin.

'Did your shopping expedition go well?'

'Yes, thanks. Monique—was very helpful.' Although Charlie was miserably aware that tongues would be wagging at Belle Robe.

'Something very strange has happened to Olivia Belaire, the Prince's fiancée. I think she must be unwell. She looked very pale.'

'Can you believe she wanted to pay for the clothes with cash? And then she didn't have enough.'

At some stage this evening she would have to confess to Rafe that she'd needed to use his money as well, but she was sure she should leave it until after the dinner.

Rafe must have noticed her distress. He gave her hand an encouraging squeeze. 'I think you need jewellery to set that dress off. Sapphires perhaps?'

Charlie gulped, touched a hand to her bare throat. Before she could answer, Rafe was summoning Jacques, his right-hand man—or perhaps his valet, Charlie wasn't sure—telling him to bring the single-strand Ceylon sapphires.

'Don't look so worried,' Rafe told her as the man hurried away. His smile was a little puzzled. 'I've never met a woman who didn't like shopping or jewellery.'

Charlie shrugged. 'If you transplant an ordinary Aussie girl into a fairy-tale European kingdom, you've got to expect a few surprises.'

Rafe's eyes gleamed as he smiled. This time he lifted her hand to his lips. 'Touché,' he murmured.

To Charlie's dismay, he left a scorch mark where his lips touched her hand.

The sapphires were promptly delivered and they were perfect to complement the simple lines of her sky-blue dress—a single strand of deep blue oval stones surrounded by delicate clusters of tiny white diamonds and set in white gold.

'Allow me,' Rafe said, lifting the necklace and securing it around Charlie's neck.

The skin around his eyes crinkled this time when he smiled. 'Perfect,' he said softly. 'Oh, and there are matching earrings. You might like to wear them as well. Take a look in the mirror.'

Charlie was a little stunned by her reflection. Who was this elegant creature?

But her cheeks were flushed pink and her fingers fumbled as she tried to fit the earrings to her lobes. Crikey, she had to calm down or she'd drop a royal sapphire and have the Prince of Montaigne down on his knees, searching for it in the thick carpet.

At last the earrings were secure.

'You look like a princess,' Rafe told her.

Yes, it was amazing what expensive clothes and jewellery could do for a girl. Charlie drew a deep breath. Tonight she would have to pretend that she was a princess-to-be. Princess Charlie or, rather, Charlotte.

What a laugh.

Any urge to laugh soon died when Rafe took her hand again. She was super-aware of his warm, *naked* palm pressed against hers, of his long fingers interlaced with hers, as he led her down the formal staircase to greet their guests.

She kept her smile carefully in place and concentrated hard on remembering everyone's names as she was introduced, but the task would have been a jolly sight easier if her pretend fiancé hadn't kept touching her. For Rafe, it meant nothing to place a hand at her elbow, on her shoulder, at the small of her back. For Charlie, it was intensely, breath-robbingly distracting.

The castle's dining room was a long rectangular space decorated with rich red wallpaper as a background for impressive paintings and gold-framed mirrors. An enormous picture window with a spectacular view of the valley took up most of the far wall. The table was exquisitely set with candles and flowers, gleaming silver and shining glassware, and everything was arranged so perfectly that Charlie could imagine a ruler had been used to align the place settings.

Throughout the delicious four-course meal, Rafe conversed diplomatically with his important guests, but his eyes constantly sought Charlie out. Many times he sent her a smouldering smile across the table.

She knew his smiles weren't genuinely flirtatious. He was playing the role of an affectionate fiancé for the sake of their guests. So, of course, she tried to remain cool and collected, to pay studious attention to the conversations all around her. Actually, she had no choice but to pay *very* careful attention, because everyone spoke rather rapidly in French and she could only just keep up with them. And she tried hard to not let Rafe's sexy smiles affect her too deeply.

Unfortunately, her body had a mind of its own, firing off heat flashes whenever her gaze met Rafe's across the table. It didn't help that she was terribly worried about the conversation she must have with him as soon as his guests had departed.

It was late when everyone finally left. Much to Charlie's amazement, the men had withdrawn to linger over coffee and cognac—she thought that kind of antiquated custom had gone out with the ark.

'This is when the men settle their important business,' one of the wives told her as their coffee was served. 'They're all so worried about this Leroy Mining Company.'

'While we just want to gossip,' said another woman, an attractive brunette.

Seeing their expectant smiles, Charlie was suddenly nervous again. Were these businessmen's wives expecting her to supply them with gossip? What would Olivia have done in her shoes? She hadn't a clue.

She didn't even know if these women had known Olivia.

'I'm all ears,' Charlie said, managing an extra-bright smile, despite the roiling tension in her stomach.

For a moment the women looked baffled.

Clearly, this wasn't the response they'd expected. They were hoping for news from her, but just when things were about to get very awkward one of the women laughed, as if Charlie had actually cracked a wonderful joke, and then the others joined in.

After that, knowing it was her duty as hostess to lead the conversation, Charlie asked them if they were coming to the ball on the night after next and it seemed that all of them were. From then on, she was fielding questions about which band would be playing on the night of the ball and whether Princess Maria or Countess von Belden had been invited.

'I'm sorry,' Charlie said. 'I've been visiting my mother In Saint-Tropez and I've left all those arrangements to Rafael.'

Somehow, she got through the interrogation without too many sticky moments. She wondered if Rafe had ensured that the guests were first-timers who hadn't met her sister. Even so, the night was an ordeal. She was battling jet lag and she was almost dropping with exhaustion. This 'princess' gig was so much harder than it looked from the outside.

She was sure Rafe must be tired, too, but after the guests left he still came to her room, as he'd warned her he must, for his expected 'nightly visit'.

'Thank heavens that's over,' he said, taking off his coat and carelessly draping it on the end of a sofa, then flopping into the deep cushions and loosening his tie and the buttons at his throat.

Charlie hadn't meant to stare as he performed this small act, but everything about the man was so utterly eye-catching. She found herself mesmerised by the jutting of his jaw as he loosened his collar, by the sudden exposure of his tanned throat, and even the way he sat with his elbows hooked over the back of the sofa, his long legs sprawled casually.

Everything about this Prince was super-attractive and manly.

Rafe caught her watching him. She looked away quickly, cheeks flaming, and then tried to make herself comfortable as she sat on the opposite sofa. But it was hard to feel comfortable with a huge weight on her mind.

There was only one thing for it, really—she had to get her worries off her chest quickly, before Rafe launched into another cosy fireside chat.

Charlie sat forward with her back straight, her hands tightly clasped in her lap. 'Rafe, I have a confession to make.'

Unfortunately, he merely looked amused, which wasn't at all helpful. 'I thought something must be troubling you.'

'Did it show tonight? I'm sorry. Do you think your guests noticed?'

'No, Charlie, relax.' He gave a smiling, somewhat indulgent shake of his head. 'It's just that I've learned to read the signs. There's a certain way you hold your mouth when you're distracted or worried, but as far as anyone else is concerned you were perfect tonight. You look very lovely, by the way.'

'Yes, you told me.' She refused to take his flattery seriously. 'It's the dress, of course.'

This brought another slow, knowing smile tilting the corners of his sexy mouth. 'Of course. We'll blame the dress. Now, what's your problem?'

Charlie's problem was the same problem that had dogged her all her life. 'Money.'

'Money?' Rafe looked understandably puzzled. 'So what's the problem exactly? You have too little or too much money?'

She couldn't imagine ever being worried about having too much money. 'Too little, of course. I'm sorry, I—'

A crease furrowed between Rafe's dark brows. 'Dare I ask about the two hundred and fifty thousand dollars I gave you? I know it's not really any of my business, but you haven't spent that already, have you?'

'Well, yes—I have—actually.' Charlie almost added an apology as she made this confession, but stopped herself just in time. She would only make matters worse if she behaved as if she were guilty. 'I'm only telling you this, because I went shopping today, and I tried to buy the clothes out of my own savings. But I didn't have quite enough, not for the shoes and boots, as well as the coat and the dresses.'

'But *you* weren't expected to pay for the clothes out of your own purse. Surely Monique explained?'

'I think she may have tried to. She said something about a St Romain account, but I wanted to pay for them, Rafe. You've already given me so much money.'

'Which you've managed to spend in forty-eight hours. That's no mean feat, Charlie.'

She had no answer for this. At least Rafe didn't ask her what she'd spent the money on. She still felt too tense about Isla to try to talk about that situation.

No doubt he assumed she'd bought a yacht or an apartment, or even that she'd used his money to pay off old debts.

A deafening silence followed her admission. In the midst of the awkwardness, she heard a *ping* from her phone, which she'd left on her bedside table.

'Do you mind if I get that?' she asked.

'By all means.' Rafe gave a stiff nod of his head and he spoke with excessive, almost chilling politeness.

Charlie knew she'd disappointed him and she might have felt guilty if she hadn't been so very anxious about her family. They must be in Boston by now. Her stomach was churning as she dashed to the phone.

CHAPTER SEVEN

RAFE KNEW IT was foolish to feel disappointed in Charlie simply because she'd dispensed with his money so easily. She was perfectly entitled to do what she liked with the cheque he'd given her.

She was fulfilling her obligations—she'd accompanied him to Montaigne and was acting as a stand-in for her sister, and that was all he'd asked of her. How she spent the money was none of his business.

Besides, he was using Charlie to his own ends, so he was in no position to make moral judgements about the girl.

To Rafe's annoyance, these rationalisations didn't help. He *was* disappointed. Unreasonably, illogically, stupidly disappointed.

Unfortunately, in the same short couple of days that it had taken Charlie to spend his payment, he'd allowed her—an unknown girl from the bottom of the planet—to steal under his defences.

Thinking back over the past forty-eight hours, Rafe couldn't believe that he'd allowed Charlie to cast a spell over him. But, surely, that must be what had happened. Somehow, despite the lectures he'd given himself, he'd allowed himself to become intrigued by the possibility that he'd discovered a rare creature—a lovely, sexy girl with genuine *heart*, who wasn't a grasping opportunist.

Foolishly, he'd decided that Charlie was different from her sister Olivia and from the other frustratingly shrewd and calculating young women in his social circles.

Rafe had been beguiled by Charlie's air of apparent naivety, and, even though he'd known that she wouldn't remain in his life beyond a few short weeks, he'd wanted to thoroughly enjoy the novelty of her company while he could.

She'd been a refreshing experience.

Or so he'd thought.

He consoled himself that he wasn't the only one who'd been hoodwinked. Even his good friend, Sheikh Faysal, had been taken by Charlie and had made remarks about her sincerity.

What had Faysal said? *'If you play your cards correctly, I'd say your Charlie could be quite an asset.'*

Ha! They'd both been conned.

* * *

Charlie was nervous as she picked up the phone. As she'd hoped, it was a message from her father.

Arrived safely. Dr Yu has assessed Isla and it's all systems go. Surgery scheduled for nine a.m. tomorrow EDT. Thank you, darling!! Love you loads, Dad & Skye xx

It was such a relief to hear from him. Almost immediately, Charlie could feel her shoulders relax and her breathing ease. Isla was in the best possible place, under the care of the brilliant doctors in Boston.

But her relief brought a welling of tears and she had to close her eyes to stop them from spilling. She drew in a deep breath, and then another.

She wasn't ready to share this news with Rafe. It was too private, too desperately scary to talk about. And it wasn't over yet. Poor little Isla still faced surgery and that was probably the most dangerous time of all.

Opening her eyes again, she caught a glimpse of Rafe's cautious, frowning expression. She supposed he'd been watching her, but as she returned to the sofa he paid studious attention to his own phone, which he slipped back into his pocket as she sat down.

For a tense moment, neither of them spoke. And then they both spoke together.

'That was a message from my father,' Charlie said.

'I was just checking the weather forecast,' said Rafe.

They stopped, eyed each other awkwardly.

'All's well with my family,' offered Charlie.

'There's more snow predicted,' said Rafe.

Charlie managed a tiny smile. 'At least I have a warm coat now.'

'Yes.'

She swallowed, wondering what on earth they could talk about when the mood was so strained. Rafe's smiles had vanished. There was no chance of regaining the warmth of last evening's conversation.

She touched the sapphires, lying cool and solid against her throat. 'Do these need to be returned to a vault, or something?'

Rafe nodded. 'I'll see to it.'

He sat, watching her with a hard-to-read, brooding gaze as she removed the necklace and the earrings and placed them back in their velvet-covered box. This time, he made no attempt to help her. Without the jewellery, she felt strangely naked.

'So, tomorrow you go to the children's hospital,' Rafe said.

Charlie nodded. 'Yes.'

'I hope that's not too much of an imposition.'

'No, I think I'll enjoy it.' She would feel closer to her family. The connection was important.

Another awkward silence fell and Rafe stared at her thoughtfully. 'I don't have any pressing appointments in the morning. I'll accompany you.'

This was a surprise—and not a pleasant one either. Under normal circumstances, Charlie wouldn't have minded. She enjoyed Rafe's company very much, probably *too* much. But now she was sure he was only going to the hospital to keep an eye on her, which meant he didn't trust her, and that possibility disturbed her.

'I'll look forward to your company,' she said quietly, knowing she had little choice.

Rafe nodded, then stood. 'The breakfast room is on the ground floor, in the south wing. I'll see you there at eight tomorrow?'

'Yes—sir.' Charlie couldn't help adding the cheeky 'sir'. Rafe was being so stodgy and formal.

He didn't smile, but one dark eyebrow lifted and a flicker of something that might have been amusement showed briefly in his eyes. He left quickly, though, with a curt *'bonne nuit'*. No kisses on the cheek tonight.

* * *

Visiting a children's hospital with a prince in tow was a very different experience from any previous hospital visit that Charlie had made.

After a polite and rather formal exchange at breakfast, she and Rafe left the castle in a sleek black, chauffeur-driven car that sported the blue and gold flags of Montaigne fluttering from its bonnet. And as they passed through the snowy streets, people turned to stare, to point and to wave excitedly. Finally, when the car pulled up outside the hospital, there was a group of reporters hovering on the footpath.

From the moment the chauffeur opened the door for Charlie, cameras were flashing and popping and she felt so flustered she almost stumbled and landed in the newly snow-ploughed gutter. The possibility of such an ignominious christening for her long red coat and knee high boots ensured that she navigated the footpath super carefully. Rafe's hand at her elbow helped.

A team of doctors, nurses and administrators from the hospital greeted them on the front steps. Charlie remembered to smile while Rafe introduced her as his fiancée, Olivia Belaire, and she did her level best to remember names as she shook everyone's hand.

Then the hospital team, plus Rafe and Charlie and the reporters, all processed inside.

Charlie leaned in to speak in a whisper to Rafe. 'Surely, all these flashing cameras will frighten the sick children?'

'They won't all be allowed into the wards,' Rafe assured her.

Indeed, as Charlie's and Rafe's coats were taken and they continued to the wards, only one television cameraman and one newspaper journalist were allowed to continue, along with the entourage of hospital staff. Charlie decided to ignore the other adults as best she could. The children were her focus and they were delightful.

Over the next hour or so, she and Rafe met such a touching array of children. Some were very sick and confined to bed, while others were more mobile and were busy with various craft activities. They talked to a little boy in a wheelchair who was playing a game on a tablet and another boy presented Rafe with a colourful portrait of himself and Olivia, both wearing golden crowns.

A little girl wearing a white crocheted cap to cover her bald head performed a beautiful curtsy for them.

'Oh, how clever you are!' Charlie told her, clapping madly. Prince Rafael, however, went one better. Responding with a deep bow, he took the little girl's hand and gallantly kissed her fingers.

The smile on the child's face was almost as huge as the lump in Charlie's throat and she knew this was a moment she would remember forever.

Of course, the cameras were flashing and whirring throughout these exchanges, but by now Charlie, glad of her jaunty polka-dot dress, had learned to ignore them. They moved on to a room that looked like a kindergarten where children were sitting at tables and busy with crêpe paper and scissors and wire.

'So what are you doing?' Charlie asked, kneeling down to the children's level.

'We're making roses,' she was told by a little girl with a bandage over one eye. 'And we made one for you!'

'Oh!'

Charlie's gratitude and praise for the pink and purple concoction were heartfelt and, although she felt quite emotional at times, she managed to keep her smile in place. Until they reached the sick babies.

Suddenly, her stomach was churning. At least there were no babies awaiting heart surgery in this ward, but she was given a warm, blanketed bundle to hold, and from the moment the little one was placed in her arms she was battling tears.

Of course, she was thinking of Isla, and of course, the cameramen zoomed in close, capturing every emotion. She didn't dare to catch Rafe's eye.

They were driving back to the castle, after morning tea with a selection of hospital staff, before Rafe commented on the experience. 'That seemed to go well,' he said, although he didn't look particularly happy.

'It was amazing,' Charlie declared firmly. 'The children were so excited to see you, Rafe. That little girl with the curtsy was gorgeous. I hope she gets better. Her doctor said he was optimistic.'

'That's good,' Rafe said warmly. 'Everyone loved you—especially the children, but you were a hit with the staff as well.'

Charlie couldn't help feeling chuffed. 'I guess I was channelling my inner princess.'

Rafe's response was an incomprehensible smile, and he looked more worried than pleased.

What was wrong? Charlie wondered with a sigh. She felt a spurt of impatience. She'd done her level best this morning. He'd said she'd done well. What more did he want?

'Why do you look so worried, Rafe? I thought

you just told me that the visit went well. I thought you were happy.'

'Of course the visit went well. You were perfect.' He gave a slow shake of his head. 'That's the problem.'

This made no sense at all. 'Excuse me?'

'You've set rather a high standard for Olivia to follow.'

'Oh.' Charlie hadn't considered this possibility. 'Are you suggesting that visiting a children's hospital might not be her cup of tea?'

'Exactly,' Rafe said grimly.

Charlie had no answer for this. She'd done what she'd been asked to do. She could do no more. 'Do you think there'll be a photo in the newspaper tomorrow?'

Rafe nodded. 'Almost certainly.'

'I wonder if Olivia will see it. Gosh, imagine how shocked she'll be.'

This brought another frown from Rafe. 'At least, she might make contact then.'

'And that's a good thing, surely?'

But his expression was still serious and thoughtful as he looked away out through the car's window. A woman and a little girl out on the street saw him and waved excitedly, but he seemed too preoccupied to notice. He didn't wave back.

Charlie, feeling sorry for them, waved instead.

* * *

The car returned to the castle and Charlie expected that Rafe would leave her now. She had no other commitments for the day, but he would almost certainly be busy. She wasn't looking forward to the next few hours of anxiously pacing the floor, trying to fill in time until she heard news from her father.

In the castle's enormous, white-marbled entrance, she hesitated, expecting Rafe to dismiss her.

Instead, he stood, tall and wide shouldered, in his large, heavy wool overcoat, with his black leather gloves clasped in one hand, watching Charlie with unexpected vigilance, almost as if she were a puzzling, troublesome child.

She was getting rather tired of trying to understand what this Prince really wanted of her. She was about to demand what his problem was when he spoke.

'Charlie, can I ask a personal question?' His manner was perfectly polite, but there was an intensity in his grey gaze that made her suddenly nervous.

In an attempt to cover this, she shrugged, rather like a teenager put on the spot by an inquisitive parent. 'I guess. What do you want to know?'

'Would you be prepared to explain why I've

seen you on the verge of tears on at least three separate occasions now?'

Her cheeks flamed hotly. 'Three times?'

'Yes,' said Rafe. 'You've been upset twice on the phone when you were speaking to your father and then today at the hospital with that tiny baby in your arms.'

'You're—you're very observant.'

'Look, I don't want to pry, Charlie,' Rafe said more gently. 'I'm fully aware that I dragged you away from your life in Sydney without really asking if it was convenient, but if something is causing you distress, perhaps I should know.'

She would burst into tears if she tried to talk about Isla, especially now with the scheduled surgery only hours away. 'I'm just a bit tense,' she hedged.

Rafe's grey eyes narrowed. 'And this tension relates to your father?'

'Sort of…yes.' It was the best she could manage. She crossed her arms tightly over her chest and hoped this was the end of Rafe's interrogation.

'Is there any way I can help?'

This was so unexpected.

Charlie had never had a drop-dead handsome man offer to help her. For a moment she was tempted to pretend that Rafe really was her fiancé, to tell him everything that was bothering her as she threw herself into his arms and sobbed on his strong, capable shoulder.

Just in time, she dragged her thoughts back to reality. 'It's kind of you to offer to help, Rafe. But, actually, I haven't talked to you about—my concerns—because I knew you might want to help. And you can't really, and if you did try, then there'd probably be all kinds of publicity and—'

'I can avoid publicity when I need to,' Rafe cut in. 'My press secretary is very good at managing these things.'

Charlie supposed this was true. There would be many times when a royal needed to avoid the press, and other times when he would welcome the attention. She supposed Rafe had been well aware that his presence at the hospital today would be a draw-card for journalists. Perhaps, Charlie realised now, he'd been using the hospital visit as some kind of bait to lure Olivia out of hiding.

This thought drew Charlie up sharply. But she didn't want to think too deeply about Rafe's relationship with Olivia. She especially didn't like to contemplate the regrettable reality that Rafe planned to go ahead with his marriage to her sister, even though he didn't love her and she clearly didn't love him.

On the other hand, when Charlie considered

what she'd been prepared to do to save Isla, she supposed Rafe might go to any length to save his country. It was all rather depressing, really.

And Rafe was still waiting for her answer.

She pulled her phone from her pocket to check the time. It was only midday, and by her calculations Isla's surgery was scheduled for three pm Montaigne time. She still had to wait hours and hours before she knew the outcome.

'I appreciate your concern,' she told him. 'But now is not a good time to talk about it.'

'When will be a good time?' Rafe persisted.

'By the end of the day.' She had no idea how she would fill in the rest of the day. 'I just wish this day would go faster,' she said, thinking aloud.

'So, why don't you allow me to divert you for an hour or so with lunch in one of our finest restaurants?'

Charlie was momentarily dumbstruck. 'Aren't you too busy?'

'Not today. I've kept my schedule clear.' A smile shimmered in his eyes as he waited for her answer.

'Will there be lots of people staring at us?'

'Not at this place. Most of Cosme's clientèle are famous in their own right. Come on, Charlie. I'll drive you there myself. Let me show you a little more of my country and one of my favourite places.'

The smile he gave her now would have done Prince Charming proud, and Charlie had to admit that the thought of a pleasant lunch in a lovely restaurant was way more appealing than pacing alone in her room and uselessly worrying.

Really, when the man invited her so nicely, she'd be churlish to refuse, wouldn't she?

Rafe drove to Cosme's in a flashy silver sports car, with the hood up against the biting cold. As far as Charlie could tell, most of the city's roads seemed to be narrow and winding, which must have made life difficult for the guys with the snowploughs. Many streets were ancient and cobbled and crowded in by tall buildings made from centuries-old stone. She was sure she would have been nervous if she'd been behind the wheel, but Rafe drove his car skilfully and with obvious enjoyment.

She wondered how often he got to taste this kind of freedom, although she supposed he wasn't ever completely free. His minders were still following at a discreet distance.

The restaurant, simply called Cosme's, was in an old building that might have once been a castle. Two pine trees stood like sentries in huge pots on either side of a bright red door, making a bright splash of welcome colour.

Inside, Charlie and Rafe, with their coats and scarves taken care of, were led up a winding stone staircase to a spacious dining area made completely of stone and warmed by a blazing, crackling fire, a proper open fire with logs. The other diners scarcely paid them any attention as they were shown to their table set in an alcove.

It was all wonderfully simple, but perfect—a starched white tablecloth, gleaming, heavy silver, a small candle in a pottery holder and another spectacular view.

Charlie was rapt as she looked out through their alcove's arched window to the pale winter sky and a steep, snow-covered mountainside. 'This is absolutely gorgeous, Rafe. Thank you for bringing me here.'

He grinned. 'The pleasure's all mine. But wait till you try the food.'

The menu was large and of course everything was in French.

'You know the menu well,' Charlie said. 'I think I'd like you to choose. What do you suggest I should try?'

'Well, you can't beat the traditional French favourites,' Rafe suggested. 'Cosme has perfected them. I'm sure you'd enjoy his *soupe à l'oignon*.'

'Oh, yes.' A proper French onion soup on a cold winter's day sounded perfect.

'But perhaps, first, you would like to try an

entrée? How about something local, like goat's cheese baked with Alpine honey?'

Charlie grinned. 'Yes, please. It sounds amazing.'

And, of course, it was totally delicious. For Charlie, who was used to cramming in a hasty sandwich at her desk in the gallery, this leisurely, gourmet lunch was the ultimate luxury.

As she tasted her first sip of a divine vintage Chablis, she couldn't help asking, 'Has Olivia been here?'

Amusement flickered in Rafe's eyes and at the corners of his mouth. 'Actually, no, she hasn't.'

She knew it was small-minded of her to be pleased about this. Surely it was shameful to have feelings of sibling rivalry for a sister you'd never even met.

Charlie's soup arrived, along with a veal dish for Rafe. The soup was wonderfully rich and savoury with a to-die-for golden, cheesy bread crust. It was so good she couldn't talk at first, apart from raving, but after a bit she encouraged Rafe to tell her more about Montaigne.

She was keen to learn more about its history and its traditions, about the mining threat and his plans for his country's future. So he told her succinctly and entertainingly about the country's history and the jewellery-making craftspeople and the famous Alpine skiers. As he talked she could feel how genuinely he loved this small principality and its people.

Charlie decided there was something very attractive about a man whose vision extended beyond his own personal ambitions. Not that she should dwell on Prince Rafael of Montaigne's attractions.

She was halfway through the soup, when she asked, in a burst of curiosity, 'What's it like to be you, Rafe? To be a prince? Does it do your head in sometimes?'

He frowned. 'My head in?'

'Does it ever feel unreal?'

He seemed to find this rather amusing. 'Mostly, it feels all too real.'

'But you must have met a lot of famous people. I guess you must have an awesome Christmas card list.'

This time Rafe laughed out loud, a burst of genuine mirth. 'Yes, I suppose it is an awesome list,' he said eventually.

'Will you add me?' Charlie couldn't resist asking. 'After all this is over?'

Any amusement in his face died. 'Yes,' he said quietly. 'If you'd like a Christmas card, I'd be happy to add you to my list, Charlie.'

The thought of being back in Australia and

finding Prince Rafael's card in the mail wasn't as cheering as it should have been.

Charlie promptly changed the subject. 'Do you ever wish you could just be plain old Rafe St Romain?'

He wasn't smiling now. 'Many, many times. But hardly anyone can have exactly what they want, can they?'

'I—I guess not.'

'That's why life's a compromise.'

'Yeah,' said Charlie softly. But today she really needed a fairy tale for Isla. 'I suppose your parents drummed that into you?'

He gave this a little thought before he answered. 'It was my granny, actually. She was a crusty old thing, prone to giving lectures. Her favourite lesson was about the need to put duty before personal happiness. I must admit, I ignored her advice for as long as I could.'

'How long was that? Until your father died?'

His eyes widened. 'You're very perceptive, aren't you?'

Charlie dropped her gaze. 'Sorry, I have a bad habit of asking nosy questions.'

But Rafe shook this aside. 'You're quite right,' he said. 'I spent far too long living the high life. It's my deepest regret that my father died not knowing if I'd give up the nonsense and step up to the mark as his heir.'

His jaw was stiff as he said this, his mouth tight, as if he was only just holding himself together. An unexpected welling of emotion prompted Charlie to reach out, to give his hand a comforting squeeze.

Rafe responded with a sad little smile that brought tears to her eyes.

'Anyway,' he said quickly. 'I don't think Granny was ever very happy herself, and she was forever warning me that I couldn't expect to be as carefree and contented as my parents were.'

'Well, at least you must be reassured to know that your parents were happy.'

'Yes.' This time Rafe's smile wasn't quite as sad. 'My mother was from Russia. She was the daughter of a count. Her name was Tanya and she was very beautiful. My father worshipped her.'

'Wow.'

Charlie thought how sad it was that Rafe, by contrast, was arranging to marry for convenience, to save his country, tying himself into a contract with a girl he didn't seem to particularly admire.

If her sister ever came out of hiding.

To Charlie this seemed like a compromise of the very worst kind.

'By the way,' he said suddenly, changing their

mood with a sudden warm smile, 'you should finish this meal with one of Cosme's chocolate eclairs. That's a happy ending you can always rely on.'

'Oh,' Charlie moaned. 'I don't think I have room.'

'We can ask for a tiny bite-size one. I promise, they're worth it.'

Charlie checked her phone again as they were getting back into the car. Rafe had noticed her checking it twice, very quickly, during the meal.

'When do you expect to hear something?' he asked.

She looked at him, her blue eyes wide, almost fearful.

'You're obviously waiting for a phone call,' he said.

She nodded sadly. 'But it won't come for ages yet. It's only just starting.'

Rafe had turned on the ignition and was about to drive off, but now he waited. Charlie had been relaxed and animated during lunch, but now she was tense and pale. 'What has just started, Charlie?'

She opened her mouth, as if she was going to tell him, and then, annoyingly, shut it again.

Rafe sat very still, but with poorly contained

patience. 'What?' he asked again, but she didn't reply.

He watched her trembling chin, knew she was struggling not to cry, and couldn't believe how the sight of her distress bothered him as much as it frustrated him. He almost demanded there and then that she tell him about it.

He certainly would have done so, if they weren't in a car on a narrow street with curious pedestrians on either side. Instead, with grim resignation, he put his foot down on the accelerator and the car roared off.

When Rafe pulled up at the castle steps a valet was waiting to open Charlie's door and to park the car. Charlie wondered if ancient dungeons had been turned into underground car parks and she might have asked Rafe about this, but the question died when he linked his arm with hers and kept a firm hold on her as they went up the steps and inside the huge front doors.

'We'll have coffee in Olivia's room,' he told the waiting Chloe.

Charlie had expected to be alone now. She wanted to focus on Isla, to send positive thoughts while she waited for news. Just in time, she remembered not to show that she minded Rafe's company. No matter how tense she was, she couldn't let him down in front of the watchful eyes of his staff. She was supposed to be his loving fiancée, after all.

She waited until they were in the lift. 'You don't need to come to my room, Rafe.'

His eyes were cool grey stones. 'But I choose to.'

He said this with such compellingly regal authority Charlie knew it was pointless to argue. She supposed she should be grateful for his company. Try as she might to send positive thoughts, she would probably end up sitting alone, unhelpfully imagining all kinds of gruesomeness as a surgeon's scalpel sliced through poor Isla's tiny chest.

Upstairs once again, she and Rafe sat opposite each other on the sofas. It was a scene that was beginning to feel very familiar, with the fire flickering, the huge window offering them its snowy view of the city and a coffee pot and their mugs sitting on the low table between them.

'Shall I pour?' Charlie asked.

Rafe nodded gravely. 'Thank you.'

The coffee was hot and strong. Charlie took two sips then set her mug down.

'How long do you have to wait for this news?' Rafe asked.

'I don't know. I guess it depends—' It was ridiculous to avoid telling him now. 'I have no idea how long it takes to operate on a not quite two weeks old baby's heart.'

She watched the shock flare in his eyes.

'This is your little half-sister?' he said, eventually.

Charlie swallowed. 'You knew?'

'I knew you had a baby sister, your stepmother's child. You visited her in Sydney before you left.'

She supposed his 'men' had told him this. 'Her name's Isla,' she said. 'She was born with a congenital heart defect.'

'Oh, Charlie.'

She held up a hand to stop him. 'Don't be nice to me, or I'll cry.'

Rafe stared at her, his expression gravely thoughtful. 'Where is this surgery taking place?'

'In America. In Boston. The surgeon is supposed to be brilliant. The best.'

'I'm sure you can rely on that brilliance,' Rafe said, and this time his voice was surprisingly gentle.

Charlie nodded. Already, after getting this sad truth out in the open, she was breathing a little more easily.

Rafe was looking at his phone. 'I guess the Internet should be able to tell us how long these sorts of operations might take.'

'I guess.' Charlie hugged her coffee mug to

her chest as she watched him scroll through various sites.

'Hmm…looks like it could take anything from two and a half hours to over four hours.'

'Oh, God.'

Poor Isla.

Rafe looked up from his phone, his gaze direct, challenging. 'This is what you wanted the money for, isn't it?'

The tears she'd warned him about welled in her eyes. Fighting them, Charlie pressed her lips together. She nodded, swallowed deeply before she could speak. 'Do you mind?'

'Mind? No, of course I don't mind. How could I mind about my money being spent on something so—so decent and honourable?' His mouth twisted in a lopsided, sad smile.

'Oh, Charlie,' he said again and his voice was as gentle as she'd feared it would be.

Oh, Charlie.

With just those two words, Rafe unravelled the last shreds of her resolve.

The tension of the past few days gave way. She could feel her face crumpling, her mouth losing its shape. Then suddenly Rafe was on the sofa beside her and he was drawing her into his arms, bringing her head onto his shoulder.

For a brief moment, Charlie savoured the luxury of his muscled strength, the reassuring firmness of his considerable chest through the soft wool of his sweater, but then the building force of her pent-up emotions broke through and she wept.

CHAPTER EIGHT

RAFE KNEW THIS was wrong. A weeping Charlie in his arms was not, in any way, shape or form, a part of his plans. But he was still trying to digest her news and its implications.

Surely he shouldn't be so deeply moved by the fact that Charlie had used his money for such a worthy cause?

It had been much easier to assume that she'd wasted it.

Now, disarmed by the truth, Rafe knew he had to get a grip, had to throw a rope around the crazy roller coaster of emotions that had slugged him from the moment Charlie hurled herself into his embrace.

These emotions were all wrong. So wrong. He'd struck a business deal with this girl, and a short term one at that. She was a conveniently purchased stopgap. Nothing more. He wasn't supposed to feel aching tenderness, or a desperate need to help her, to take away her worries.

The problem was—this girl had already become so much more than a lookalike body double that he could parade before Montaigne like a puppet. Charlie Morisset was brave and unselfish and warm-hearted and, when these qualities were combined with the natural physical attributes she shared with her beautiful sister, she became quite dangerous. An irresistible package.

But somehow Rafe had to resist her appeal. He'd made his commitment. He'd chosen Olivia as his fiancée. They'd signed a contract, and even though she'd disappeared he was almost certain she was playing some kind of game with him and would turn up when it suited her.

Meanwhile, Charlie was being predictably sensible. Already, she was pulling out of his arms and gallantly drying her eyes, and making an admirable effort to regain her composure.

She gave him a wan smile and they drank their cooling coffee. Outside, the afternoon was turning to early twilight.

Rafe stood and went to the window, looking out. 'It's not snowing. Perhaps we should go for a walk. All the lights are coming on, so it should be quite pleasant, and you still have a long time to wait.'

He was sure a long walk in fresh air and a chill wind were what they both needed. Anything was safer than staying here on the sofa with Charlie.

The temptations were huge, overwhelming, but only a jerk would take advantage of her when she was so distraught.

'Won't you be mobbed if you try to walk out on the streets?' Charlie asked.

'It's not too bad at this time of the year. With an overcoat and a woolly cap and scarves, I can more or less stay incognito.' He smiled at her. She should have looked pathetic, so wan and puffy-eyed from crying, but she brought out the most alarming protectiveness in him. He held out his hand to haul her to her feet. 'Come on.'

Charlie had the good sense to recognise that Rafe's suggestion of a walk was the right thing to do under the circumstances. Sitting here, feeling sick and scared, was not going to help anyone in Boston. She could change into jeans and a sweater, and she'd bought a warm hat, as well as a scarf and gloves, so she would be well protected against the cold.

Besides, it was incredibly considerate of Rafe to put up with her weeping and to devote this entire day to her. The least she could do was accept his kind suggestion.

Outside, the sky and the air were navy blue, on the very edge of night. Lamplight glowed golden, as did the lights from shops and houses, from the headlights of cars. Pulling their hats low and winding their scarves tighter, they set off together, with Charlie's arm linked in the crook of Rafe's elbow.

Ahead stretched the long main street that led from the castle. On either side were pastel-coloured buildings from different eras, mostly now converted into shops, hotels and restaurants.

'This section of the city is called Old Town,' Rafe told her. 'New Town starts on the far hill-side, beyond that tall clock tower.'

He seemed to enjoy playing tour guide, pointing out the significance of the clock tower and the statue of his great-great-grandfather in full military regalia, complete with medals. When they rounded the next corner and came across a small cobblestoned plaza with a charming statue of a young boy with a flock of goats, Rafe told her the story of the goatherd who was Montaigne's national hero.

'His name was Guido Durant,' Rafe said. 'He acted as a kind of unpaid sentry up in the high Alps. When the Austral-Hungarians were making their way through a narrow pass in winter, planning to invade our country, Guido dug at rocks and stones and managed to get a snow slide going. It turned into a full-blown avalanche and blocked their way. Then he ran through the night all the way to the castle to warn my great-great-grandfather.'

'So he's Montaigne's version of William Tell?' Charlie suggested.

Rafe shot her a surprised smile. 'You know about William Tell?'

'Of course. My father used to love telling me that story. He used to play the opera, too, turning the music up really loud. It's very dramatic.'

'Yes, it is,' Rafe agreed. 'It was one of my father's favourite operas, actually.'

'My father's, too.' Charlie laughed. 'Crikey, Rafe, we do have something in common after all.'

'So we do,' he said quietly and his grey eyes gleamed as their gazes connected, making Charlie feel flushed and breathless. For a crazy moment, she thought he was going to do something reckless like haul her into his arms and her skin flashed with heat, as if she'd been scorched by a fireball.

Then the moment was over.

They walked on and the smell of cooking reached them from the many cafés, but they weren't very hungry after their substantial lunch.

Montaigne's capital city was packed with charm. Charlie loved the cobblestoned alleys, the arched doorways with fringes of snow, the shop windows with beautifully crafted wares, including jewellery that Rafe told her was locally made from gemstones found right here in the Alps. She especially loved the glimpses into cosy cafés where laughing people gathered.

'Can you ever go into places like that?' she asked him, as they passed a group at a bar who were guffawing loudly, obviously sharing a huge joke.

He shrugged. 'I have a few favourite cafés where I like to meet with friends.'

'Thank heavens for that.'

'Are you worried about me, Charlie? You think I'm not happy?'

'Well, no, of course not,' she said, which wasn't true. She wasn't sure that anyone who believed life was a compromise could really be happy.

His smile was complicated as he tucked her arm more snugly in his.

They went on, past a tenth-century cathedral, which, according to Rafe, had beautiful frescoes in its cloisters, past a museum of culture and local history, a monastery where a choir was practising, sending beautiful music spilling into the night.

Once again, Charlie imagined herself at some point in the distant future, when she was middle-aged and married to some respectable, ordinary Aussie man, telling others, perhaps her children, about this magical mountain kingdom that she'd once visited with a handsome prince.

She didn't suppose anyone would believe her.

Rafe's phone rang twice during their walk, but the calls seemed to be business matters that he was able to deal with quite quickly. Just once, Charlie checked her phone. There wasn't any news about Isla. She had known there wouldn't be, but she'd had to check anyway.

Always, throughout the walk, her fear about her baby sister sat like a heavy rock in her chest.

They were almost back at the castle, passing a market stall that sold arts and crafts and local honey, when Charlie heard the ping of a text message.

Her heart took off like an arrow fired from a bow. She came to a dead stop in a pool of yellow lamplight, felt sick, burning, and was almost too scared to look at her phone.

Rafe stood watching her, his eyes brimming with gentle sympathy. He smiled, a small encouragement.

Terrified, Charlie drew the phone out from the depths of her overcoat pocket. She was so scared she could hardly focus on the words.

Isla out of surgery and Dr Yu is happy. She'll be in Intensive Care for about four days, but so far all good. Love, Dad xxx

'Oh!' She wanted to laugh and cry at once.

Unable to speak, she held up her phone for Rafe to read the message, but she was shaking so badly, he had to clasp her hand tightly to steady it before he had any chance of reading it.

'She made it!' His cry was as joyous as Charlie's and he looked so relieved for her that she couldn't help herself. Launching towards him, she threw her arms around his neck, and hugged him hard, and then, impulsively, she kissed him. On the mouth.

No doubt it was an unwise move for an Australian commoner to kiss a European crown prince in such a public place. Fortunately the Crown Prince didn't seem to mind. In fact he gathered the commoner into his arms, almost crushing her as he held her tightly against him, and he returned her kiss with breath-robbing, fiery passion.

It seemed fitting to go into a café to celebrate the good news. Rafe took Charlie's hand and showed her a place tucked away in a back street that seemed to be carved out of stone like a cave. As they went inside, another welcoming fire burned in a grate, rows of bottles and glasses reflected back the cheerful light, and although there were one or two excited glances and elbow nudges from curious customers, they didn't hassle the newcomers as they perched on tall wooden stools at the bar.

Charlie's head was spinning.

Calm down, girl, it was just a kiss.

But it wasn't just *any* old kiss. She knew she'd never been kissed with such intensity, such excitement, had never experienced such a soul-searing thrill.

But he's a prince, a jet-setter, a playboy. He's had masses of practice. A kiss like that means nothing to him.

Could she be sure? It had felt very genuine.

Yes, that's the problem.

She had to stop thinking about it. Had to concentrate on Isla.

None of this would have happened if Isla had been well.

Rafe ordered *vin chaud*, which proved to be a delicious mulled wine laced with cinnamon, cloves and juniper berries.

'Here's to Isla,' he said, clinking his glass against Charlie's.

'Yes. To Isla.' Charlie lifted her glass. 'Hang in there for another four days, kiddo.' She took a sip. 'Wow, this is amazing.'

'It's a favourite drink with the skiers,' Rafe told her.

'I can certainly understand why.' Charlie drank a little more. 'I've never been skiing.'

He pretended to be shocked. 'That's something we'll have to remedy.'

The thought of skiing with Rafe was thrilling, but Charlie doubted they would have time. Apart from the hospital visit this morning, today had been unusually free of engagements. The private time alone with Rafe had been an unexpected bonus, but she knew he had commitments that were bound to keep him very busy. And tomorrow evening, there was to be the grand ball.

Charlie had never been to a ball and the very thought of it made her nervous. She would have to wear that beautiful, and incredibly expensive, pale green gown, and her schedule tomorrow included appointments with a hairdresser and a beautician.

It was best not to think about that tonight while they lingered over their *vin chaud.*

Eventually, they continued on their way, stopping to buy hot roasted chestnuts from a stall on a street corner and eating them from a paper cone. When they reached the castle, Rafe ordered a light supper to be brought to Mademoiselle Olivia's room.

In the lift, Charlie gave herself a stern lecture.

Forget about that kiss. You started it, remember?

Yes, and Rafe was just being kind.

Kind? Really?

That's probably how a playboy expresses kindness.

It won't happen again.

Delicious mini-pizzas arrived, topped with caramelised onions, black olives and Gruyère cheese. And there were cherries for dessert along with a pot of the most divine hot chocolate.

As they enjoyed their supper, Rafe filled Charlie in about the important dignitaries who would attend the ball tomorrow evening.

'You won't be expected to know everyone,' he assured her. 'But I'll ask Mathilde to give you a list with photos, so you can at least learn some of the names.'

'That would be helpful, thank you.' Charlie remembered something else that was bothering her. 'What about the dancing?'

'Ah, yes.' Rafe frowned. 'I should have thought about that earlier. Can you waltz?'

'No, not really. I mean—we learnt a little ballroom dancing at school and I've watched people waltzing on TV. I know it's basically one-two-three, one-two-three, but—' Charlie grimaced awkwardly. 'I don't suppose there'll be any disco dancing?'

Rafe smiled. 'There'll be some, I should imagine. But you'll be expected to know how to waltz.'

'Could Olivia waltz?'

'Yes. She's quite a good dancer, I must admit.'

Damn. 'Any chance we could have a bit of practice before tomorrow night?'

'Of course,' Rafe said without hesitation.

It was silly to feel so self-conscious, almost blushing at the thought of dancing in his arms, their bodies lightly brushing.

'You don't want to start worrying about that now, though,' he said. 'I'll see you tomorrow evening, say an hour early, before the ball, and we can have a little practice. Your room's carpeted, so it won't be the same as dancing on a proper dance floor, but at least we can run through the basics. I'm sure you'll pick it up very quickly.'

'OK. Thank you.'

The charming meal was a lovely end to a perfect day. All too quickly, it seemed to Charlie, it was time for Rafe to leave. He rose from the sofa, taking both her hands in his and drawing her to her feet.

Her heart began a silly kind of drumming.

Stop it.

'Thanks for giving up so much time to be with me today,' she said. 'It's been—' She was about to tell him it had been wonderful, a stand-out, red-letter day that she would never forget. But perhaps over-the-top enthusiasm wasn't wise at this point. It was time to remind herself that this was only a role that she was being paid to fulfil.

Instead of gushing, she said carefully, 'I appreciated your company. It was—very nice.'

'Very nice?' Rafe repeated in a tone that implied she had somehow insulted him.

'Well…yes.'

Leave it at that, Charlie. Too bad if he's disappointed. It's important to keep your head.

Perhaps Rafe understood. He responded with a courteous nod. 'I enjoyed the day, too. You're great company, Charlie, and I was very pleased to share the good news about your little sister.'

It felt strained to be so formal after the closeness they'd shared today, but Charlie told herself that this new, careful politeness was desirable. This was how matters must be between herself and the Prince. Even though Rafe was still holding her hands, it was time to retreat from being overly familiar.

It was time to remember the reality of their situation. She was only a temporary fill-in until Olivia was found—or until Olivia returned of her own accord.

Charlie was pleased to have her thoughts sorted on this matter, but then Rafe spoiled everything by clasping her hands more tightly and holding them against his chest.

Big mistake. She could feel his heart beating beneath her palm.

In response, her own heart was hammering. She tried to ignore it.

'You're a very special girl,' he said with a wry smile. 'Note I said *special*, not just very *nice*.'

'Special is open to interpretation,' Charlie said more curtly than she meant to.

'So it is.' Rafe lifted her hands to his lips. 'Perhaps you'd prefer nice?' Keeping his grey gaze locked with hers, he kissed her hand, and his lips traced a seductive path over her knuckles.

Of course, Charlie's skin burned and tingled wherever his lips touched, and she knew what would come next. At any moment, Rafe would take her into his arms again and he would kiss her. Already, she could imagine the exquisite devastation of his lips meeting hers.

She had never wanted a kiss more, but she had to remember why this shouldn't happen.

'D-don't play with me, Rafe.'

He frowned as he stared at her, trying to read her.

Time seemed to stand still.

And poor Charlie was already regretting her plea, as the wicked vamp inside her longed for Rafe to go on kissing her hands, kissing her mouth, kissing any part of her that took his fancy.

But he was letting her hands go. 'Forgive me, Charlie. I did not intend to take liberties.'

It was ridiculous to feel so disappointed. Charlie knew she should be relieved that her message had got through to the playboy Prince.

'I'll see you at breakfast in the morning,' he said politely. 'Sleep well.'

With another formal bow, he backed out of the room, but the blazing signal in his eyes was anything but formal, and there was no way Charlie could miss its message. She only had to say the word and Rafe would drop the formalities. In a heartbeat, she would be in his arms, in his bed, discovering what it was like to make love to a prince. All night long.

Somehow, she stood super still until the door closed behind him.

Oh, help. Now she would have the devil's own job getting to sleep.

CHAPTER NINE

NEXT MORNING, WHEN Charlie went down to the breakfast room, she half expected to find that Rafe had left already, but he was still at the table, polishing off a croissant stuffed with smoked salmon and scrambled eggs. After a restless night, she felt a little uncertain about his mood, but he greeted her with a smile.

'*Bonjour*, Olivia.'

'*Bonjour,*' she responded carefully, knowing there were servants within hearing range.

Rafe immediately shot a pointed glance towards the newspaper on the table beside him.

The headline jumped out at Charlie.

OLIVIA LOOKS FORWARD TO MOTHERHOOD!

She gasped, caught Rafe's eye. He gave a helpless shrug.

The headline was accompanied by a photo

of Charlie standing in the hospital's nursery in her new black and white polka-dot dress, holding the snugly wrapped baby and gazing at it wistfully, while Rafe watched with a smile that might easily be interpreted as fond.

The accompanying story began: *Olivia Belaire's motherly instincts were on clear display yesterday when she and Prince Rafael visited Montaigne's Royal Children's Hospital...*

Charlie skipped the rest of the story to check out another smaller headline.

ROYAL-IN-WAITING BRINGS CURTSIES AND SMILES.

The photograph beneath this caption showed Charlie and Rafe in the children's ward, standing close together, grinning with delight and applauding as the little girl in the crocheted cap performed her curtsy.

Charlie wondered what Olivia would make of these stories, if she saw them.

'Are you happy with this?' she asked Rafe, holding up the paper.

'My press officer's happy, so that's the main thing.' Over his coffee cup, he smiled at her again. 'You did well. I told you that yesterday. Everyone loved you.'

Charlie supposed she should be pleased, but

she didn't really know how to feel about this. It was all too weird, and now that she wasn't quite so stressed about Isla she found herself wondering about her other sister. Olivia.

What was the real reason for Olivia's decision to take off? Would these photos of her double bring her out of hiding? If so, when would she show up? How would that scene play out?

Charlie couldn't help wondering if Rafe had thought this charade through properly, considering all possible consequences.

Then again, Charlie knew that for herself there was only one possible outcome. As soon as Olivia returned, Charlie's role at Montaigne would be over, which meant she could be gone from here within a matter of days.

Hours?

In no time she would find herself back in Sydney, back in her little flat that she'd decorated so carefully. She would be reunited with Dolly, her cat, and she'd see all her friends again and resume her role at the gallery. Once again she would be living in hope that she might sell her father's paintings for an enormous sum.

Taking her seat at the breakfast table, Charlie wished she felt happier about the prospect of going home. It didn't make sense to feel miserable about going back to her own world and her old life, the life that had been perfectly satisfactory until she'd been so suddenly plucked from it.

Her low mood was annoying. Puzzling, too. She knew she couldn't have fallen in love with Rafe in such a short space of time. And anyway, even if she had, foolishly, lost her head, it couldn't be an emotion of the lasting kind.

She was simply dazzled…starstruck. This man and his castle and his beautiful principality were all part of a fairy tale, after all. This world wasn't real—not for an everyday average Aussie girl.

'Is everything all right?' Rafe asked her in French.

Charlie blinked and it took her a moment to compute his simple question. 'Of course,' she said at last. 'I was just wondering when a certain person might be found.'

'Oh, yes, I know.' He frowned. 'It's very frustrating.'

Charlie suspected that Rafe might have said more, but a young man with carefully slicked-back hair, dressed in a pristine white shirt and black trousers, appeared to pour her coffee and to politely offer her warmed platters of food awaiting her selection. She copied Rafe and took a croissant with scrambled eggs and a little smoked salmon.

'I'm going to be busy for most of today,' Rafe told her as the young man hovered to pour his second cup of coffee and to make sure Charlie had everything she needed. 'But I've arranged for Mathilde to give you that VIP guest list with the photos.'

'Thank you.'

'And I won't forget our arrangement to meet prior to the ball. I think seven o'clock should give us enough time.'

'Yes, I'll make sure I'm ready.' Charlie was rather looking forward to their dancing lesson.

Rafe nodded. 'There's nothing else you need today?' And then almost immediately, he answered his own question. 'Of course, you'll need jewellery for tonight.'

'Well, yes, I suppose I shall.'

'What colour is your gown?'

Charlie thought about the beautiful gown hanging in her wardrobe. She remembered the slinky sensation of the fully lined satin and the way it had clung and rippled about her body as she moved. Now that the ball was drawing close, she was a bit self-conscious about wearing it in public.

'It's a sort of pale green.' she said. 'Not an apple green, a pale—I don't know, a smoky green, perhaps?' The colour was hard enough to describe in English, but trying to do so in French was almost impossible. Charlie knew she was making a hash of it. 'I think Monique may have called it sea foam, or something like that.'

'Sea-foam green?' Rafe's grey eyes widened. He didn't look impressed.

Charlie lifted her hands in a helpless gesture. 'Don't worry, Rafe, it works. That colour shouldn't suit me with my blue eyes, but it seems to.'

'I'm sure it's very beautiful, Char—Olivia.' It was the first time Rafe had ever slipped up with her name. Was it a sign that he was nervous about her performance tonight? This would be her first real test in front of all the most important people in Montaigne. She was beginning to wish that she'd chosen a nice safe white or blue dress.

But then, to her surprise, Rafe said, 'I can't wait to see you wearing it.' And he sent her a smile so smouldering it should have been illegal. Charlie was too busy catching her breath to reply.

'I imagine,' he said next, 'that pearls and diamonds might be best suited to your sea foam.'

'Yes,' Charlie agreed, very deliberately calming down, despite the exciting prospect of wearing royal pearls and diamonds. 'I think they'd be perfect.'

'Good. I'll arrange to have them sent to your room before seven.'

'Thank you.'

* * *

It was yet another day of new experiences. Charlie had been to hair salons before, of course, and had once indulged in a spray tan at a beauty salon in Sydney. But she'd never been to a suite of salons as grand and luxurious as the place Rafe's chauffeur delivered her to for today's appointments.

She'd certainly never been so pampered. By the end of the day she'd been given a warm oil body massage and a winter hydrating facial, as well as a manicure, pedicure and eyebrow wax—and of course, there had been a beautiful healthy lunch that included a ghastly looking green smoothie that was surprisingly delicious.

Charlie's hair had been given a special conditioning treatment, too, and her scalp had been massaged, her curls trimmed.

'Oh, my God, Olivia! Your hair has grown so much since your last cut!'

Charlie merely nodded at this. 'It grows fast,' she agreed, crossing her fingers under her cape.

After a short but intense discussion among the hairdressers about the Prince's expectations for the ball, Charlie's hair was styled into a glamorous updo. And then her make-up was applied. She'd been rather nervous about this. She was worried that the make-up would be too heavy, that it would involve false eyelashes and she'd end up looking like a drag queen. She wanted to be able to recognise herself when she saw her reflection.

There was no problem with recognition, however. In fact, the results were amazing. The girl in the mirror was the same old Charlie, but her skin now had a special glow, a feat she had never managed before without making her nose shiny. Her eyes seemed to have acquired an extra sparkle and glamour. Her hair was glossy, her curls artistically tamed. The result was faultless.

Charlie was a little overawed by this newly refined and sophisticated version of herself. She *almost* felt like a princess. She quickly stomped on that thought before it took root.

By seven o'clock the names and faces on the supplied list had all been memorised—Charlie had tested herself several times—and she was dressed and ready. The sea-foam dress still looked good, she was relieved to see.

It was sleeveless with a scooped neckline and an elegant, low cowl back, but it was the slinky way the dress flowed, responding to every subtle movement of her body, that made it so special.

She had never gone out of her way to draw attention to herself, but she knew this was the sort of dress that would let everyone, male and female, know she was in the room. The addition of Rafe's heirloom pearls and diamonds—delivered by his valet, Jacques—completed her transformation. She had expected a necklace and earrings, but there was a tiara as well, which Jacques kindly helped her to secure.

When the valet left she was rather stunned when she saw herself in the mirror. The dress was a dream, the make-up dewy-perfect. The elegant up-sweep of her hair and the gleaming pearls and sparkling diamonds of the tiara had combined to create the perfect image of a princess.

Charlie Morisset was in for a *big* night.

For Rafe's sake, she only hoped she could get through it without making too many blunders.

Rafe was due at any moment and, rather than waiting for him to knock, Charlie opened her door, ready for his arrival. As she did so she heard strange noises—blasts and ripples of music floating up the staircase from the grand ballroom on the lower floor. Trumpets, clarinets, saxophones and flutes. The band was warming up.

Excitement and anticipation pinged inside her and she drew a quick, steadying breath. Not that it did her any good, for a moment later Rafe stepped out from a doorway across the hall and she completely forgot how to breathe.

He was dressed in a formal black military

uniform with gold braid on his shoulders, a colourful row of medals and a diagonal red and gold sash across his broad chest. His dark hair, as black as a raven's wing, gleamed in the light of overhead chandeliers and he looked so handsome and so splendidly royal that Charlie's knees began to tremble.

Drop-dead gorgeous had just been redefined.

It didn't help that Rafe had come to a complete standstill when he saw her, or that his smile was replaced by a look of total surprise.

The trembling in Charlie's knees spread to the rest of her body and she might have stumbled if she hadn't kept a death grip on the door handle. She wished that Rafe would say something—*anything*—but he simply stood there, staring at her with a bewildered smile.

After an ice age or two, she managed to speak. 'Are you coming in?'

Rafe nodded and she stepped back to allow him to enter her room. 'That's an amazing uniform,' she said, hoping to ease the obvious tension. 'You look very—regal.'

'And you look, *literally*, breathtaking, Charlie.' He turned to her and gave a shaky smile as he let his burning gaze ride over her from head to toe and back again. 'You're going to steal the show tonight.'

She managed to smile. 'You had your doubts about the sea foam.'

Rafe shook his head. 'I knew you would choose well.'

'I'm glad it's OK, then.'

'OK? *C'est superbe. Magnifique!*'

As Charlie closed the door Rafe stepped towards her, reaching for her hands. His grey eyes were shining so brightly they'd turned to silver. A knot in his throat moved as he swallowed. 'My dear Charlie,' he whispered, taking her hands in his and drawing her nearer. 'I think I've made the most terrible mistake in bringing you here.'

Charlie's throat was suddenly so painfully tight she could barely squeeze out a response. 'Why is that?' she managed at last.

Rafe's mouth twisted, as if he was trying for a smile, but couldn't quite manage it. 'I don't know how I'll ever be able to let you go.'

Oh, Rafe.

She wanted to weep, to melt in his arms, to acknowledge the unmistakable emotions that eddied between them, to give in to the sizzling chemistry. But a warning voice in her head reminded her that she had to be sensible.

In less than an hour they were expected to host a royal ball that would be attended by all the local VIPs, including Rafe's enemies. Being seen at such an occasion was the very reason she'd been brought to Montaigne. Decorum was required. Dignity, not passion.

She shook her head at him. 'Don't pay me compliments, sir. Not now. You'll make me cry, and that will spoil my make-up, and I'm sure it cost you a small fortune.'

A rueful chuckle broke from him. 'I've never met a girl so worried about money. But, OK, no more compliments.'

'Good.' Although Charlie feared that a dancing lesson with Rafe would be even more dangerous than his compliments.

'I'll have to kiss you instead,' Rafe said next. 'Perhaps there is no make-up here?'

Before she quite realised what was happening Rafe touched his fingers to her bare shoulder and, before she could gather her wits to stop him, he pressed his warm, sexy lips to the same patch of skin.

Charlie gasped as his lips brushed her in the gentlest of caresses. Her skin tingled and flamed. The blood in her veins rushed and zapped.

'Or perhaps here?' Rafe murmured as he pressed another kiss to Charlie's neck and caused a starburst of heat, just above the pearls and diamonds.

'What about here?' he whispered, and Charlie had no choice but to cling to him, grabbing at the stiff cloth of his jacket, closing her eyes, as he kissed the sensitive skin just beneath her ear. And then gently nibbled at her earlobe.

She tried to tell herself that he was just being a playboy, and she might have believed this, if she hadn't already seen that shimmer of a deeper emotion in his eyes.

And now she was only too painfully aware of the truth about her own feelings. She was in love with this man. Totally. Utterly. Deeply.

It didn't make sense, she knew it was wrong, but she couldn't help it. From the moment she'd left Australia, this Prince had charmed every cell in her body. Right now, she was powerless.

'You do crazy things to me, Charlie.' Rafe's arms tightened around her and his voice was hoarse and breathless as he whispered close to her ear. 'You make me want to forget everything, throw off my responsibilities. You make me want to believe in your fairy tales.'

Oh, Rafe. Charlie's throat ached with welling tears. *What have we done?*

And now, his grey eyes were fierce, burning with an intensity that was almost scary, as he ever so gently touched the backs of his fingers to her cheek. 'I've never really believed in love till now. But my problem was that I'd never met the right girl. And now I have. Now I want to believe.'

Emotion and longing rioted through Charlie. She thought she might burst.

Rafe's sad smile was breaking her heart. 'Is it safe to kiss your lips?' he whispered.

She knew she should step back, tell him no. If he kissed her mouth, heaven knew what else might happen.

But it was so hard to be sensible. To her dismay, she heard herself say, 'I have a new lipstick for touch ups.'

Idiot.

It was all the invitation the Prince needed. Slipping his arms around Charlie's waist, he gathered her closer, and now she could smell the expensive cloth of his jacket, the light cologne on his skin.

His lips found hers and her heart seemed to burst into flames. She tipped her head to access the dizzying pleasure, and worried, fleetingly, that her tiara might slip, but this worry and all others were shoved aside as Rafe's lips worked their magic. His kiss was all-seeking and possessive, commanding every shred of her attention.

Happiness and hunger in equal parts rose through Charlie like a bubbling geyser. She no longer cared that she'd fallen under this Prince's spell. She would happily hand him her heart on a platter.

With unforgivable ease, he had won her completely and, as his kiss deepened deliciously, a soft moan of deepest pleasure escaped her.

But the moan was cut short as the door burst open.

A woman's voice yelled, 'What the hell's going on?'

CHAPTER TEN

OLIVIA.

The woman bursting through the door couldn't be anyone else. An exact replica of Charlie, she was dressed in a magnificent white fur coat and elegant, knee-high white boots. She looked stunning. Stunning and very angry.

Ignoring Rafe, the newcomer directed her glaring gaze straight to Charlie. 'What the hell are you doing here?'

'Olivia.' Rafe had gone pale, but he managed to sound calm. 'What impeccable timing you have.'

Slamming the door behind her, Olivia flounced past them into the room and flung her expensive copper-toned handbag onto the nearest sofa. 'Don't talk to me about timing, Rafe. I deserve an explanation. What's going on? What's *she* doing here?'

Hearing herself called 'she', Charlie felt weirdly dislocated from this scene, as if a real-life version of herself had taken centre stage, and she was an invisible spectre watching on.

'I'll explain in due course,' Rafe told her coolly. 'Just as soon as you've apologised for your disappearance. You knew full well that you'd cause me enormous problems by taking off like that, without warning or explanation. You knew my country was left in grave danger.'

Olivia pouted. 'I always planned to come back.'

Rafe looked unimpressed. 'It would have been helpful if you'd informed me of your plans.'

This brought a shrugging eye roll from his fiancée. Olivia reminded Charlie of a petulant teenager.

Rafe was standing with his shoulders braced, his eyes wary but determined. 'Where have you been, Olivia?'

'In Monaco.' She gave another offhand shrug, as if her answer was obvious. 'I needed to—see someone.'

Charlie could sense the fury mounting in Rafe as he glared at her sister.

Olivia pouted back at him. 'You haven't explained what she's doing here.'

'Isn't it obvious? You know very well that I needed a fiancée. A *visible*, *available* fiancée.' Rafe turned to Charlie and his grey eyes now betrayed a mix of sadness and resignation. With a courteous nod to her, he said, 'Charlie, allow me to introduce you to your sister, Olivia Belaire. Olivia, this is Charlotte Morisset, from Australia.'

If Charlie had dreamed of being greeted by Olivia with a sisterly hug, she was promptly disappointed. Olivia didn't so much as offer a handshake, let alone a kiss on the cheek. Instead she lowered herself onto the arm of the nearest sofa, letting her fur coat fall open to reveal a tight, tiny, copper silk dress.

Then she crossed her legs, which looked rather long and sexy in the knee-high white boots. 'Yes,' she said airily. 'I know who she is. I rang my mother and got the whole story from her.'

'So you never knew about me either?' Charlie couldn't help asking. 'Not till today?'

'No.' As she said this, Olivia finally lost some of her belligerence. 'It was a terrible shock to see those photos of you at the hospital.'

Charlie could well believe this. She remembered her own shock and disbelief back in Sydney when Rafe had first shown her the photo of the girl on the beach in Saint-Tropez. It was astonishing to think that she and this girl had shared their mother's womb, had been babies together until their parents' divorce.

She wondered what had caused the bust up.

Had the birth of twins been the final blow for an already shaky relationship between a woman who loved the high life and a dreamy, impoverished artist? She saw her puzzlement reflected in Olivia's blue eyes. No doubt her sister was asking herself similar questions.

'How on earth did you find her?' Olivia asked Rafe.

'My men were searching high and low for you, Olivia, but you were very good at keeping under the radar. And then we were sure we'd found you in Sydney.'

'But that's ridiculous. Why on earth would I go to Australia?' Olivia said this as if Australia were still a penal colony.

'We have beaches, too,' Charlie couldn't help snapping. 'Beaches and snowfields and casinos. Sydney's not Mars, you know?'

Rafe sighed, shifted his cuff to check the gold watch on his wrist. 'Anyway, we don't have much time to thrash this out now. There's a grand ball due to start in less than thirty minutes.'

'Yes, so I gathered from all the fuss downstairs. Obviously, that's why you two are all dressed up.' Olivia's eyes narrowed as she studied Charlie in her finery. Then she smiled archly and gave another shrug. 'Well, I'm back now.'

'For how long?' asked Rafe.

'For as long as you need me, Rafey. I've sorted everything out with my boyfriend.'

This brought a further stiffening of Rafe's shoulders, a deeper frown. 'You never mentioned a boyfriend.'

Olivia gave yet another nonchalant shrug. 'I know. Andre and I had a fight just before I met you. Well, a bit of a tiff. I'd gone home to Saint-Tropez in a huff.'

Rafe glared at her now and Charlie could imagine what he was thinking—that Olivia had agreed to the fiancée role in a fit of spite to get back at her boyfriend. How awful.

'But surely this fellow's not prepared to let you marry me?' Rafe said.

Olivia's jaw jutted stubbornly. 'He is, actually. He's prepared for me to complete the terms of our contract.'

So there was a contract. It was all signed and sealed. Charlie felt ice water pool in her stomach. For her, then, this was it. Her exit line. She was no longer needed.

As if to confirm this, Olivia shot another glance Charlie's way. 'It was good of you to fill in for me, Charlotte.'

'It was *indeed* very good of Charlie,' Rafe cut in coldly. 'She dropped everything to help me out.'

'Yes, but I'm sure you paid her very well.'

This brought another glare from Rafe as Olivia sat there in her fur coat and boots, with one crossed leg swinging, while she smiled at him shrewdly. He looked as if he would have liked to shake her, but instead he clasped his hands behind his back and stood with the stiff, unhappy dignity of a prince who had been schooled by his granny to put duty before personal desires.

Rafe should have known this would happen. It was no doubt typical of Olivia to turn up at the very worst possible moment, but he couldn't believe he'd made such a serious error of judgement and recklessly chosen her in a moment of panic. He was a fool, the very worst version of a thoughtless idiot.

And now, what about Charlie? What the hell had he been thinking when he'd started kissing her? Damn it, he hadn't merely kissed her, he'd been seducing the poor girl, when he'd known all too well that he had absolutely no right to toy with her emotions.

There was no point in trying to excuse himself now, by trying to pretend that Charlie was simply irresistible. Sure, he'd found himself daydreaming about her constantly and, yes, he was desperate to make love to her. Even though they'd only shared a kiss or two, he'd sensed an exciting wildness in Charlie that had only fired his own desire to greater heights. Their few, sweet kisses had been just enough to tease him, to give birth to a deep and painful longing, the whisper of a promise, a burning question without any answers.

It had been such a delightful surprise to discover that a girl who looked so much like Olivia could be so very different beneath the surface. Beyond the beauty, there'd been so much to *love* about Charlie—her openness, her sudden surprise questions, her selfless concern for her baby half-sister. But all these differences should have warned him to protect Charlie, not to expose her.

Olivia might have been out of sight, but, although Rafe had only known her for a painfully brief time, he'd been almost certain that she would turn up again, when she was good and ready. And he'd also been fully aware that he'd signed a contract with her, a contract which he now had no choice but to honour.

The terms of their contract were clear. Rafe was paying Olivia a sum of money that was enormous, even by his standards, to take on the role of his wife. At a future date, when Pontier and the Leroy Mining Company threats were satisfactorily resolved, Olivia would then be free to divorce him. No doubt, she would go back to this boyfriend, who would enjoy sharing her profits. By then, Rafe should supposedly have found a more suitable bride.

These plans had all been so clear and watertight.

Before he'd walked into a certain art gallery in Sydney.

And now… Rafe couldn't bear to see the hurt and shock and disappointment in Charlie's eyes. He knew full well that he'd caused her this pain. He'd played with her feelings unforgivably.

He'd gambled recklessly with his own feelings as well. In a moment of weakness he'd allowed himself to imagine—or to hope, at any rate—that life wasn't the compromise he'd always believed it to be, and that Charlie's happy endings were indeed possible.

Fool.

Now there was no way to resurrect this situation without making things worse for Charlie.

'So.' Olivia was smiling smugly as she finally rose from her perch on the arm of the sofa. 'It's obvious from the little scene I've so recently interrupted that you two have grown quite pally.' The smile she sent Rafe and then Charlie was condescending in the extreme.

Charlie had no choice but to ignore the piercing pain in her heart. She tried to hide her distress with a defiant tilt of her chin. But she didn't dare to catch Rafe's eye.

'But like it or not, it's time for me to relieve you of your duties, Charlotte,' Olivia said next. 'I'm sure you'll agree that *I* should attend tonight's ball with Prince Rafael.'

No-o-o! Just in time, Charlie jammed her lips tightly together to hold back her cry of protest.

It didn't really help that Rafe looked angry, as if this new possibility hadn't occurred to him.

'That's not very practical,' he told Olivia. 'As you can see, Charlie's all ready to—'

But Olivia, having thrown Charlie a quick look that was probably meant to be pitying, stopped him with a raised hand. 'If I'm to be your wife, Rafe, I'm the one who needs to meet all these important people tonight.'

Rafe's eyes narrowed. 'In theory, that's true. But the ball's about to begin,' he said. 'And Charlie has gone to a great deal of trouble.'

'I'm sure she has, and, yes, she looks beautiful,' Olivia admitted grudgingly. 'And I suppose I should apologise if my arrival has been a trifle inconvenient, but *I* want to go to the ball. I believe I should go. It doesn't make sense for her to carry on as my double now that I'm here.'

Olivia didn't quite stamp her foot, but she might as well have. The insistence in her voice was equally compelling.

Rafe, however, could match her stubbornness. 'Olivia, be reasonable. It's too late.'

'Oh, for heaven's sake, Rafe, don't tell me you're taking her side.'

'It's not a matter of taking sides.'

Charlie couldn't stand this debate. 'It's not too late,' she shouted.

The other two turned and stared at her, both obviously surprised that she'd spoken up.

'It's not too late,' Charlie said again, hoping desperately that her voice wasn't shaking. 'It won't take me long to get changed.' She knew there was no other choice, really.

Olivia was right. Rafe had made a legal and binding commitment, and, as his future wife, Olivia should be at the ball tonight, mixing with Montaigne's VIPs.

Charlie knew that Rafe was aware of this. He'd only protested because he felt sorry for her.

And that was rubbish.

There was no point in feeling sorry for her. She'd completed her commitment and now she was free. Free to leave Montaigne. Why prolong the torture by attending a silly ball and dancing with a ridiculously handsome prince, spending an entire night at his side, pretending to be his chosen bride?

All those touches and smiles from the Prince would be sure to completely break her already shattered heart. She'd been stupid to allow herself to get so hung up on him. Now, there really was no valid reason for her to stay another moment in these clothes, living the lie.

'I can be undressed in a jiffy,' she told them. 'At least we know Olivia and I are the same size.'

Rafe looked grim.

Olivia looked satisfied and ever so slightly triumphant.

Charlie lifted her head even higher. 'If you'll excuse me—'

With that, she retired to her adjoining bedroom, walking very deliberately with her shoulders back and her head bravely high, closing the door quietly but firmly behind her.

'Would you like a hand?' Olivia called after her.

'No, thanks!'

Don't cry, Charlie warned herself as she sank back against the closed door. *Don't you dare waste a moment on crying. You'll only look ridiculous with make-up streaking down your cheeks and you'll slow down this whole horrible, inevitable process.*

Best to get it over with.

Drawing a deep, shuddering breath, she stepped away from the door and turned her back on the full-length mirror with its taunting reflection. Methodically, she began to undress.

First she unpinned the tiara and set it on the quilted bedspread. The pearl and diamond earrings and necklace came off next and Charlie placed them carefully back in their box, which she set on the bed beside the tiara. She kicked off her silver shoes, set them neatly on the floor at the end of the bed.

With the removal of each item, she could feel herself stepping further and further away from Rafe. She tried not to think about the exciting ballroom downstairs, the musicians on their special dais, the white-coated waiters with their silver trays of drinks, the enormous flower arrangements, the brilliant chandeliers, the enormous ballroom floor polished to a high sheen. Not to mention the long staircase where she and Rafe had planned to descend, her arm linked with his, as they went to receive his official guests.

Unlike Cinderella, she wouldn't have to leave before midnight—she wouldn't make it to the ball at all.

She knew she was foolish to feel so disappointed. She'd only ever been a stopgap, a fill-in. It was time to get out of the dress.

The zipper for the ball gown was discreetly hidden within a side seam beneath her left arm.

Charlie carefully slid the zipper down, then gently, somewhat awkwardly, eased out of the gown.

The silk-lined satin whispered and rustled about her as she dragged it over her head, taking care not to smudge the shiny fabric with her make-up. She really could have done with help for this manoeuvre, but eventually she got the dress off without a lipstick smear, or a split seam.

She arranged the gown on a hanger on the wardrobe door. The pale sea-foam satin shimmered, making her think, rather foolishly, of mermaids. Hadn't there been a poem she'd learned long ago about a forsaken merman?

One last look at the white-wall'd town...

For heaven's sake! Her mind was spinning crazily, throwing up nonsense. *Stop it!*

She let out the breath she'd been holding, collected the white towelling bathrobe from a chair where she'd left it, pulled it on and tied the sash at her waist. She took the carefully chosen lipstick from her evening bag and set it on the bed, where Olivia could find it, beside the jewellery.

There. It was done. She was no longer a princess, not even a pretend one. She was Charlie Morisset once more.

Unfortunately, this thought brought no sweet rush of relief.

Resolutely, she returned to the bedroom door and opened it.

Rafe and Olivia were still there, more or less where she'd left them. They were standing rather stiffly and neither of them looked happy and Charlie wondered what they'd been saying to each other.

'Over to you, Olivia,' she said quietly.

'Thank you, Charlotte.'

'Would you like me to help you?'

'I—' Olivia hesitated. 'I'm not sure. I'll call out if I need you.'

'OK.'

As the door closed on her sister, Charlie rounded on Rafe, needing to speak her piece before he could try to apologise, as she was sure he would.

'It's OK,' she told him quickly. 'I'm fine about this, Rafe. Honestly. If I'd gone to the ball, I probably would have made a hash of things, getting people's names wrong, making mistakes with my French, standing on your toes when we were trying to waltz.'

His sad smile was almost her undoing. 'You've been very gallant, Charlie, but I do owe you an apology.'

Why? For kissing me?

She would break down if he tried to apologise for that.

'Save it for later,' she said as toughly as she could. 'I'll be fine here in my room, if someone could send me a little supper.'

'Of course.'

'I'm assuming I can keep this room for tonight?'

'Most definitely. I wouldn't dream of asking you to leave. There are other rooms that Olivia can use. And I'll arrange for a special meal to be sent up for you.'

'Your staff will be gobsmacked to realise there are two of us.'

'Perhaps, but they're trained to be very discreet. Just the same, I'll have a word with them to smooth the waters.'

Charlie nodded. 'Thank you.' She looked down at her bare feet beneath the white bathrobe. After the pedicure, her toes were looking especially neat and smooth with pretty, silvery green nail polish. She supposed it had been a whimsical choice to wear nail polish to match the sea-foam dress when her toes wouldn't even be seen. Anyone would think she'd been planning to wear glass slippers.

Hastily, she lifted her gaze from her feet, only to realise that Rafe was staring at them, too. Feeling self-conscious, she rubbed one bare foot against the other as she tried to banish stupid thoughts about what might have happened tonight, after the ball, if she and Rafe had opted to pick up where their kiss had left off.

Before she could stop her reckless thoughts, they rushed away, and she was picturing the two of them in bed—her bed, his bed—it didn't matter whose bed—and it wasn't just her feet that were bare.

Stop it!

'Have you had news about Isla this afternoon?' Rafe asked.

Desperately grateful for the change of subject, Charlie smiled. 'I was able to speak to my dad,' she told him. 'Isla's still doing well. Dad said the doctors were very happy with her progress and he sounded so relieved. It was lovely to hear the happiness in his voice.'

Rafe nodded. 'That's very good news.'

'It is.'

She was wondering what they might talk about next, when a voice called from inside.

'Charlotte, can you give me a hand with this tiara?'

'Coming,' Charlie called back, and she hurried to her sister's assistance, without another glance in Rafe's direction.

She'd thought she was prepared for the sight of Olivia in the ball gown, in *her* ball gown, but the reality was even more startling than anything she'd imagined.

Olivia was stop-and-stare gorgeous. The softly shimmering gown clung to her body in all the right places, the deep cowl back was divine, and the pale fabric rippled sensuously as she moved.

'Wow!' Charlie said. 'I hope you like the gown.'

Olivia grinned. 'It's adorable, isn't it?'

'Yeah,' Charlie said flatly.

'A good choice. Is it from Belle Robe?'

Charlie nodded.

'Monique's brilliant.' Olivia grinned. 'I'm looking forward to another shopping spree. But right now I need a couple of pins to anchor the ends of this tiara.'

'Yes, I can do that.' Charlie obliged, marvelling as she did so at the incredible similarity between her hair and her sister's. It was amazing now, up close, to see that Olivia's tresses were the exact same colour of wheat, had the same amount of curl, were the same texture. She was suddenly overwhelmed by the enormity of their connection.

They'd come from the same egg. For nine months they'd nestled together in the same womb. She wondered who had been born first. Had her father been present for their birth?

Olivia, however, was busily applying another layer of Charlie's lipstick. 'Well,' she said. 'I think I'm ready.'

'You look lovely,' Charlie told her. 'Like a proper princess.'

'That's the general idea.' Olivia picked up the beaded silver evening bag, popped the lipstick inside.

Charlie blinked, desperate to hide any hint of tears as her lookalike headed for the door.

Just before she reached it, Charlie had to ask, 'Why did you do it, Olivia? When you already had a boyfriend, why did you agree to marry Rafe?'

Her sister smiled archly. 'For the same reason as you, my dear Charlotte. For the money, of course.'

CHAPTER ELEVEN

CHARLIE DIDN'T WATCH Olivia and the Prince as they left for the ball. Excusing herself quickly, she retired to her room. Tears threatened, but she gave herself a mental shake. She'd known from the start of this mad adventure with Rafe that it would all end with her sister's return, so it made absolutely no sense to feel sorry for herself.

But she wasn't going to beat herself up either. Sure, she'd been reckless. Any way you looked at it, agreeing to pretend to be a foreign prince's fiancée was pretty damn crazy. Many would call it foolish in the extreme.

But Charlie consoled herself that at least her original motives hadn't been merely mercenary, and Isla was out of the woods, so that was a huge positive. Her mistake had been getting sidetracked by all the trimmings—a handsome and charming prince and his beautiful castle and his gorgeously romantic Alpine principality.

And at least she'd learned one or two things

from this wildly unreal experience. She no longer believed any of that nonsense about fairy tales and happy endings. Sadly, Rafe's depressingly realistic theory was correct. Life *was* a compromise.

For Charlie Morisset, it was time to remember who she really was. An everyday, average girl from Down Under. And a poor one at that.

Right, come on, girl. Get a grip on reality. Deep breath.

When the first strains of waltz music drifted up from the ballroom, she turned on the television. She'd hardly watched any TV since she'd arrived in Montaigne, but tonight she curled up on the sofa in front of the fire and scrolled through channels till she found a romantic movie, so old it was in black and white. It was also in French, without subtitles, but Charlie could just keep up.

She refused to think about the laughter and the music and glamour downstairs and she refused to give a moment's thought to Olivia dancing in Rafe's arms. The film was very good, and she managed to remain deeply engrossed until a knock at the door signalled the arrival of her dinner.

'Please, come in,' she called.

Guillaume appeared, bearing a heavily laden tray and looking deeply distressed. 'His Highness ordered a special dinner for you, *made-moiselle*.'

Charlie smiled bravely. 'How kind of him.'

Guillaume set the tray on the coffee table, then gave a deep bow. He looked as if he might have been going to say something of great importance, but after standing with his mouth open for a rather long and awkward moment, he swallowed, making his Adam's apple jerk nervously, then said simply, *'Bon appetit, mademoiselle.'*

'*Merci*, Guillaume.' For his sake, Charlie replied with as much dignity as she could muster, while seated in her bathrobe, and she waited until he'd gone before she examined her meal.

As the door closed behind him, she lifted the lid on a small casserole dish and was greeted by the tantalising aroma of beef in red wine with herbs and mushrooms. On checking out the other covered dishes, she found *foie gras* and toast fingers, and wedges of several different cheeses. Yet another little dish housed crème caramel.

Oh, and there was a selection of Belgian chocolates! And as if these luxuries weren't enough, there was a bottle of Shiraz *and* an ice bucket with champagne, plus the appropriate glasses.

I could get well and truly plastered.

It was a tempting thought. Charlie could have

used a little cheering up, although the last thing she wanted was to leave the castle with a hangover. Even so, it was very thoughtful of Rafe to make sure she had such a wonderful selection.

And it didn't help at that moment, to remember the Prince's many kindnesses.

Rafe wasn't just the hunkiest guy she'd ever met. He really was, despite his princely status and his many regal responsibilities, the most thoughtful man she'd ever known. She was used to her dad's vagaries, and none of her boyfriends had been especially considerate or caring. Rafe, however, had gone out of his way to make sure she'd thoroughly enjoyed her short stay in his country.

And then, of course, there were his kisses…

Would she ever forget the way he'd kissed her tonight, taking such exquisite care not to mess her make-up? All those delicious sexy kisses to her neck, to her throat and ears…

Until their caution gave way to passion.

Oh, such blissful passion!

No wonder she needed to cry.

It was hours later when Charlie's phone rang. She had fallen asleep on the sofa at some unearthly hour, having found a second movie to watch while drinking yet another big glass of the deliciously hearty red wine. It took her a moment to find her phone among the scattered dishes on the coffee table. Her fingers finally closed around it just as it was due to ring out.

'Hello,' she said sleepily.

'Charlie, I'm sorry if I've woken you. It's Dad.'

A chill skittered through her. Suddenly terrified for Isla, Charlie sat up quickly, heart thumping. 'Yes, Dad? How's Isla?'

'Isla's OK,' her father said quickly. 'Actually, she's better than OK. She's coming out of ICU tomorrow.'

'Oh, that's wonderful.'

'Yes, it is. I'm not ringing with bad news, Charlie. It's good news, rather amazing news, actually. It's about my paintings.'

'Really?' Charlie was waking up fast. 'Don't tell me you've sold one?'

'Not just one painting, Charlie. I've sold five!'

'Oh, wow! How?' She was wide awake now. 'Tell me all about it.'

And, of course, her dad was more than happy to recount his amazing story. 'I happened to meet this fellow here in Boston called Charles Peabody. He works here at the hospital, some kind of world-famous surgeon, actually, absolutely loaded. Anyway, Dr Yu introduced us, just out of politeness, but it turns out Peabody's wife was born in Sydney, so he has a bit of a soft spot for the place. *And* he's apparently something of an art collector.'

'That was very handy.'

'Wasn't it? It's as if my stars were all aligned. Anyway, we were yarning and I happened to mention my paintings.'

'As you do.'

Her father laughed. 'Of course. Anyway, Peabody was really interested. Afterwards, he got in touch with his New York dealer, who was able to show him my paintings online. And he fell in love with the painting of the alley. You know the one—you've always liked it, too—*View from Cook's Alley*?'

'Yes, of course,' said Charlie. 'That's always been my favourite.'

It was a remarkable painting, she'd always believed. It showed a view down a steep, narrow alley that had grimy, old buildings on either side that served as a frame for a sparkling view of Sydney Harbour. The slice of the bright blue sky and sunlit water with pretty sailing boats and the curve of the Harbour Bridge made a startling contrast to the narrow dark alley with dank gutters, a stray cat and newspapers wrapped around the bottom of a lamp post. 'That's so fantastic, Dad. I always knew someone would realise you're a genius. I'm so happy for you. I hope this Peabody fellow is paying you top dollar?'

'Top dollar? You wouldn't believe the sum the dealer managed to sell it for. I still can't bring myself to say it out loud, in case it breaks a spell or something.'

Charlie chuckled. No wonder she was superstitious. She got it from her dad.

'But the amazing thing is,' her father went on, 'the dealer's already sold four more paintings to American collectors—in New York, in Seattle, San Francisco and New Orleans. After all these years, it seems I've become an overnight international success.'

Charlie's laugh was a little shaky. She was feeling teary again. 'That's so fantastic. Totally deserved, of course.'

'Thanks, darling.' Her dad's voice sounded a bit choked now. 'And I mean that. I owe you heartfelt thanks, Charlie. I'm pretty sure I would have fallen by the wayside without you there to prop me up more than once.'

Charlie had to swallow the lump in her throat before she could speak. 'And these sales might never have happened if it wasn't for Isla,' she said.

'Correction. They wouldn't have happened if it wasn't for you, Charlie. I don't know how you found that money, or who the kind benefactor was, but we're so, so grateful.'

Now she gripped the phone harder, fighting more tears.

'You know what this means, don't you, love?' her father said next.

'Your money worries are over.' At last. Finally. 'Dad, you so totally deserve this.'

'But it also means I can pay you back for Isla's operation, and you can pay whoever you borrowed the money from.'

'Yeah.' Charlie knew it made no sense to be sobered by this prospect. The timing was perfect. Now she wasn't only free to leave Montaigne, she would also be able to hand the money back to Rafe, even though he didn't expect it, and her ties with him would be severed. Neatly. Cleanly. Permanently.

If only she could find a way to feel happy about that.

As dawn broke over the castle, Rafael St Romain paced the carpeted floor in his private suite. He was bone weary, but he was also bursting with impatience. Except for the night of his father's death, this night of the Grand Ball had turned out to be the most unexpectedly significant and pivotal night of his life. As a result, he hadn't slept a wink.

It had all begun quite early in the evening. The business of greeting the long line of guests was just coming to an end, when the head of police, Chief Dameron, stepped up to Rafe, leaning close to his ear.

'We've got him,' he whispered excitedly.

Rafe immediately knew who the man was referring to. It had to be Montaigne's Chancellor, Claude Pontier.

The news was exhilarating, but Rafe hid his surprise behind a frown. 'You've made an arrest?'

'Better than an arrest, Your Highness. Would it be possible to have a private audience?'

The last of the guests had been presented, so Rafe excused himself, murmuring his apologies to Olivia, before retiring with his police chief to a small salon. There he was given details of the good news. The police had intercepted several important phone calls from Claude Pontier and now they had irrefutable evidence of his corrupt dealings with the Leroy miners who threatened Montaigne with so much damage.

Chief Dameron handed Rafe a document. 'And here is Pontier's signed resignation.'

This time Rafe's jaw dropped. 'He's resigned as Chancellor? Already?'

'Yes, Your Highness.' Chief Dameron allowed himself a small smile. 'Given the man's options, resignation seemed to be his wisest choice.'

Rafe was elated, of course, but he didn't like

to think too deeply about the techniques his police might have used to persuade the Chancellor to roll over so quickly. Dameron was a gracious and gentlemanly old fellow, but Rafe could almost imagine him threatening Pontier with some ancient punishment for treason, possibly involving menacing machinery and dark, unpleasant dungeons.

'Well,' he said, shaking off these thoughts as the good news sank in. 'We'll need to appoint a new Chancellor.' Which also meant he had the chance to appoint a citizen who was unquestionably sympathetic to his country's best interests.

The police chief nodded. 'If you'll pardon my forwardness, Your Highness, might I make a suggestion?'

'By all means.'

'I'd like to highly recommend the Chief Justice, Marie Valcourt, as someone very suitable to be the next Chancellor.'

'Ah, yes.' Rafe smiled. Marie Valcourt was indeed an excellent choice. Apart from her inestimable legal skills, she was fiercely loyal to Montaigne. Her family's history in this region went back almost as far as his own. Besides, he rather liked the idea of a woman as Chancellor. His father would possibly roll in his grave, but it was time his country moved with the times.

'I'm sure we can trust Marie to act with Montaigne's best interests at heart,' he said.

'I'm certain of it.' Chief Dameron's smile broadened. 'If this were medieval times, Justice Valcourt would be donning blue-grey armour and standing at the city gates, sword in hand.'

Rafe laughed. 'She's a wonderful champion of our cause, that's for sure. A first-class suggestion, Chief.'

After that, it was almost bizarre how quickly everything had turned around. By midnight, while the Grand Ball continued with music and waltzing and an endless flow of champagne, Rafe had consulted in private chambers with his minsters and, with their consent, he'd spoken at some length to Justice Marie Valcourt. Within a matter of hours, he had appointed her as Montaigne's new Chancellor.

It had been well after midnight when the final guests eventually left. Of course, Olivia had known that something was in the wind, but fortunately she'd been happy enough to spend the evening dancing with just about every available male.

Olivia had done this with very little complaint, for which Rafe was excessively grateful, and afterwards, as he explained the new situation to her, he couldn't blame her for being instantly wary.

'So what does this mean for me, Rafe?'

'Chancellor Valcourt agrees that the constitutional requirements regarding my marriage are totally out of date and unnecessary,' Rafe told her. 'There's to be a special meeting of Cabinet tomorrow to repeal the old law. I'm assured it will be passed, without contest, which means—'

'I'm no longer needed here,' Olivia supplied.

He nodded. 'If that's what you wish, yes, you are free.'

'I can tear up our contract?'

'Yes, you can.'

'But I can keep the money?'

He suppressed a weary smile. 'Of course.'

Olivia brightened instantly. 'That—that's very kind, Rafe.'

'No, it's you who has been kind,' he assured her. 'I'm very grateful to you for stepping up to the plate. My country would have been in deep trouble without your help.'

'And Charlotte's help, too,' Olivia said with unexpected generosity. Then her eyes narrowed as she shot Rafe a cagey glance. 'I suppose my sister will go home now as well?'

'I suppose—'

Rafe paused in his pacing and stood at the window, looking out over the familiar view of snowy rooftops, which were only just visible in the pre-dawn light. It was almost eight. A reasonable hour, surely? He didn't think he could wait much longer before he went to Charlie's room.

Of course, he wanted to ask her to stay.

All night, during the ball, throughout the political manoeuvres and the diplomatic tensions, Rafe had been battling with thoughts of Charlie and their interrupted kiss. He couldn't get the honeyed taste of her kisses out of his mind. He kept remembering the exquisite pleasure of holding her in his arms, her breasts pressed against his chest, her stomach crushing against his hard arousal.

He kept hearing the soft needy sighs she'd made as she wound her arms more tightly around him, driving him insane with the knowledge that she was as ready as he was.

Now that he'd had hours to pace impatiently, his memories of her were at fever point. Rafe desperately needed more of Charlie. He needed her spontaneity and responsiveness. He'd been waiting all night.

He was dizzy with wanting. He wanted her. Now.

At eight-fifteen Rafe left his room, his pulses drumming crazily as he crossed the carpeted hallway to Charlie's door. He knocked quietly, and held his breath as he waited for her response.

There was no sound from within.

Perhaps she was still asleep? He waited a little longer, listening intently for the smallest sounds, but Charlie's suite was fully carpeted, so her footsteps would almost certainly be silent.

After what felt like an age, but was probably no more than thirty seconds, Rafe knocked again, more loudly this time.

There was still no response. He remembered the two bottles of wine he'd sent to her room last night. Perhaps she'd been a little too indulgent and was sleeping it off?

He called, 'Charlie? Charlie, are you awake? It's Rafe.'

When there was still no response from within he began to worry. Swift on the heels of his worry came action. Pushing the door open, Rafe marched into the sitting room, where Charlie had dined last night. It was all very tidy now. No sign of her meal. Even the cushions on the sofas were plumped and in place.

The door to Charlie's bedroom was closed, however. Rafe crossed to it and knocked again. 'Charlie?'

Again, there was no answer and he felt a fresh stirring of alarm.

'Charlie!' he cried more loudly, pushing open the door as he did so.

The bed was empty.

In fact it was neatly made up. And there was no sign of her belongings. Thoroughly alarmed, Rafe flung the wardrobe doors open. The long red coat, the blue dinner dress and the black and white polka-dot outfit from Belle Robe were still hanging there—but not the ball gown, which was now in Olivia's possession. All Charlie's other clothes and her suitcase were gone.

He knocked on the door to the en-suite bathroom, then opened it. Again, it was empty and cleared of Charlie's things.

Dismayed, Rafe went back to the bedroom. And that was when he saw the small folded sheet of white paper on the snowy pillow. With a cry, he snatched it up.

He hardly dared to read its contents. By now, he had no doubt that the news wouldn't be good.

His fears were quickly confirmed.

Dear Rafe,

Goodbye and thanks so much for everything. Your country is beautiful and you've been a wonderful host. It's been an amazing experience.

My bank will be in touch to repay you

the money in full. I wish you and Olivia every happiness.

Oh, and I've borrowed your chauffeur. Apologies for the inconvenience,
Charlie xx

If Rafe had thought he'd cared about Charlie before this, now the true weight of his feelings crashed down on him. The thought of losing her was as painful as cutting his own heart out with a penknife.

He couldn't possibly let her go without making sure she understood how he felt.

He wasted no time on a second reading of her note. Grabbing his phone, he speed-dialled his chauffeur.

'Tobias, where are you?'

'Good morning, Your Highness. I have just driven Mademoiselle Morisset to Grenoble.'

'You're there already?'

'Yes, Your Highness.'

Rafe cursed. It was rather telling that Tobias had referred to Charlie by her correct name—*Morisset*. 'I gave you no such instructions,' he barked.

'Forgive me, Your Highness, but you told me to make myself available to the *mademoiselle* at all times.'

This was damn true, Rafe remembered now,

through gritted teeth. And perhaps he shouldn't be surprised that Charlie had won over his staff. 'So you're already at the airport?'

'I am, sir.'

'And Mademoiselle Morisset has already booked her flights.'

'I believe so, Your Highness.' After a small silence. 'Yes, she has.'

Damn.

As Rafe disconnected he was already racing through the castle. He had no choice but to drive his own car down the mountain as quickly as possible. No matter what risks were involved, he couldn't let Charlie simply fly away.

It was freezing when Charlie stepped out of the car at Grenoble airport. She almost wished she'd brought her lovely new overcoat with her, but she was determined to leave behind everything that meant she was in any way indebted to the Prince.

Now, she knew that Tobias had been speaking to Rafe on the phone. In other words, Rafe knew where she was, so on the off chance that he might, for some crazy reason, try to follow her, she shouldn't linger over farewells.

She needed to get away, to get safely home to Sydney and to put this whole heartbreaking experience behind her.

'Thank you, Tobias,' she said as he set her suitcase on the footpath. 'I really appreciate everything you've done for me, especially your skilful driving down those steep snowy roads.'

'Thank you, *mademoiselle*. It's been my pleasure.'

'I hope Prince Rafael won't be too angry with you for bringing me here this morning,' she said.

Tobias shrugged. 'Don't give it another thought. Would you like me to help you with your suitcase?'

'No, thank you. It has wheels. It's as easy as pie.' She pinned on a smile as she held out her hand. 'Goodbye, then, Tobias.'

'*Adieu, mademoiselle.* I wish you a safe journey.' To Charlie's surprise, a look of genuine warmth shone in the chauffeur's eyes as he smiled. 'I and the rest of the castle staff will miss you, *mademoiselle*.'

Miss me? This was so unexpected, Charlie felt a painful lump in her throat. Her vision grew blurry. Why, oh, why was she so susceptible to people saying nice things about her?

She managed a shaky, crooked smile. 'I'll miss you, too. I've had a wonderful stay in your country.'

Then quickly, before she made a total fool of herself, she grabbed the handle of her suitcase, yanked it into its extended position, gave a hasty wave, and hurried away, dragging the wobbling suitcase behind her as she went through the airport's huge sliding glass doors.

Rafe drove as quickly as he dared down the steep, winding mountain road. Of course, there were princely responsibilities that he should have been attending to this morning, but right now finding Charlie before she boarded a plane was far more important than anything else.

He couldn't bear to think that Charlie might slip away before they had a proper conversation. Charlie knew nothing about the way his entire situation had changed overnight. He had to tell her that he was free from the pressure to marry her sister. More importantly, he had to tell her the truth that lay in his heart.

Unfortunately, it was going to be a damned difficult conversation to get right. Rafe needed Charlie to understand the true strength and depth of his feelings for her.

Some might say this was an unreasonable expectation, given that Rafe hadn't really understood these feelings himself until this morning. It was only when he'd read Charlie's note and realised that he was going to lose her that he'd faced a moment of terrifying truth. Everything had been suddenly, frighteningly clear.

Charlie Morisset was desperately important to his future happiness.

Rafe had known many women—all glamorous, beautiful or charming in their own way—but he'd never known a woman like Charlie. Charlie was not only beautiful and sexy, but she was honest and genuine and caring and funny and kind.

In just a few short days, she had become so much more than a girlfriend Rafe wanted to bed. She'd become a rare and real friend. She'd answered a deep need in himself that he hadn't even realised existed. Until now.

Unhappily, he knew it would be asking a great deal to expect Charlie to believe in the truth of his rapid transformation. It would be especially difficult when time was so pressing. Charlie had every right to tell him to take a flying leap.

Rafe cursed aloud, but it wasn't the particularly sharp bend in the roadway that bothered him. It was the harrowing possibility that he might let Charlie go.

And yet…if he was honest, he had to admit that he had used the girl to his own ends, with very little regard for her finer feelings. Now he wanted to make amends, but there was only the briefest window of opportunity to set things right.

As the Prince of Montaigne spun the steering wheel back and forth, negotiating yet another set of hairpin bends at the fastest possible speed, he tried to practise what he must say to his no-nonsense, straight-shooting Australian.

If only it could be as easy as it was in the movies when a guy chasing a girl could win her with a simple *I love you.*

CHAPTER TWELVE

CHARLIE FELT CALMER once she'd emerged from the long queue in Customs and was safely in the departure lounge. In less than an hour now she would be on a flight home to Sydney via Paris, this time without a diversion to Dubai and a handsome sheikh's residence.

She bought herself a cappuccino, a croissant and a paperback novel. She chose a murder mystery, rather than a romance. It would probably be years before she could bear to read another romance. She now knew better than to believe in happy ever after.

Settling at a table in the corner of the café, she took a sip of her coffee and opened the paperback with a great sense of purpose.

Focus, girl, focus.

The story was set in the American Midwest, thousands of kilometres from anywhere Charlie had ever been. It was midsummer, apparently, and the hero cop had a doozy of a hangover.

There was a body lying in the middle of a cornfield. Flies were buzzing around it.

Charlie sighed and closed the book. She wasn't normally squeamish, but this morning she wasn't in the mood for blood and gore. Problem was, she wasn't in the mood for any form of entertainment, really.

Her mind, her whole body, felt numb. She broke off a corner of her croissant. She hadn't had any breakfast and she should have been hungry, but even the sweet pastry filled with strawberry jam seemed tasteless.

It was as if her senses had been dulled. She had left Montaigne and sent herself into self-imposed exile, and nothing would ever be the same again.

No Rafe.

Forget him.

But how could she forget him? How could she forget the whole prince-Alpine-castle fairy tale? The gorgeous lunch at Cosme's. The walk with Rafe through the snowy streets, holding hands. The look in his eyes when he saw her in the ball gown. His kiss.

Oh, help, that kiss.

How was a girl supposed to get over something as life-changing as that?

Heading to the opposite hemisphere is supposed to help. Aren't distance and time supposed to cure all wounds?

Yes, once she was back in Sydney, surrounded by everything that was familiar and dear, she'd feel so much better. All she wanted was for this flight to be over.

She needed to be home.

Rafe's car skidded to a halt in the airport car park. As he leapt from the driver's seat an attendant glared at him. Rafe pressed several large notes into the man's beefy hand. 'Be a good fellow and park this for me.'

'But—'

'This is an emergency.'

Without waiting to see the attendant's reaction, Rafe took off on foot, racing into the airport terminal, heedless of the surprised stares of staff and travellers. He was a man on a mission, a desperate mission as far as he was concerned. He *had* to see Charlie. He couldn't let her go back to Australia without speaking to her, without making sure she understood that everything about his situation had changed.

Mathilde had tracked down Charlie's flight and had texted him the details. Now, in the middle of the busy airport, he scanned the list of flights that were preparing for departure.

Already, Charlie's flight was boarding. A chill swept through him. He still had to wrangle with Security and Customs, had to persuade them to let him get through to her.

But he would do this. He was the Prince of Montaigne. With luck, someone at the Customs gates would recognise him, but if that didn't happen he would wave his royal passport in their faces and make them understand.

He would do whatever was necessary to stop that plane.

Flying home was going to be a very different matter from the flight in Rafe's luxurious chartered jet. Charlie was crammed into economy class beside a little Japanese man who seemed to go to sleep as soon as he sat down and a very large American businessman who only just managed to get his seat belt done up.

Wedged between them, Charlie tried to look on the bright side. She could watch back-to-back movies if necessary and, if she didn't sleep, at least she would be home inside twenty-four hours and then she could sleep for a week.

She had hoped to keep Rafe out of her thoughts, but she found herself wondering if he was awake yet. No doubt he'd slept in quite late after the Grand Ball, but he might be up by now.

Had he seen her note? Would he be upset that she'd left without saying a proper goodbye?

Or would he simply move Olivia back into her room and get on with his life?

This possibility was so depressing, Charlie picked up her novel and tried again to read, forcing herself to concentrate on the words on the page and to ignore the questions in her head, the heavy weight in her chest.

'Miss Morisset?'

Charlie had actually made it to page three—after having read the second page several times—when she heard her name. She looked up to see a pretty, auburn-haired flight attendant fixing her with a wide-eyed, fearful stare, almost as if she suspected Charlie of being a terrorist or something equally horrifying.

Charlie tried not to panic. 'Yes?' she said.

'Could you please come with me?' the attendant asked.

A shaft of white-hot panic shot through Charlie. What could possibly have gone wrong now? Was there a mistake with her ticket? She'd never bought a plane ticket using her phone before. But surely a problem would have been picked up at the airport desk. Not now, at the last moment.

Despite her profuse apologies, the large American wasn't happy about getting out of his seat to make room to let Charlie past. She tried to ignore all the curious stares of the other passengers, but her cheeks were flaming as she followed the flight attendant back down the long narrow aisle, through business class and first class, where people were already sipping champagne, to the very front of the plane.

'What's the matter?' she asked, when the attendant finally stopped at the plane's front door. 'Is there a problem with my ticket?'

'There's someone here who needs to speak to you,' the girl said, nodding towards the air bridge. Her eyes were bigger than ever, and a couple of other attendants were also staring at Charlie.

Crikey, anyone would think she was a celebrity or something. Or had something terrible happened? Was it a message from her father? Were the police trying to contact her?

Stiff with fear, Charlie forced her feet to move forward, through the doorway. Then she saw the tall, dark-haired, masculine figure in a long charcoal overcoat and her knees almost caved.

It didn't make sense. What was he doing here? Was she dreaming?

'Charlie!' A huge smile lit up Rafe's handsome face as he stepped forward, reaching for her hands.

'Wh-what are you d-doing here?'

'I had to see you. I couldn't let you go.'

'Why? Is something wrong?'

'No, not at all. Everything's fine, in fact. Very fine indeed. That's why I had to see you, to let you know.'

And suddenly, standing in the air bridge, holding her hands tightly in his, Rafe told her a crazy story about his Chancellor and some Chief Justice and an overnight change in Montaigne's laws. He said that he and Olivia weren't going to marry after all, and now he wanted Charlie to know how he really felt about her.

Her head was spinning.

'I haven't slept all night for thinking of you,' Rafe said.

Charlie hadn't slept for thinking about him, but she wasn't about to admit that now when her mind was made up. She'd put too much hard thinking into reaching this point.

Now she didn't know whether to laugh or to cry. This was like something out of a dream—or a nightmare; she wasn't sure which.

'I want you to stay.' Rafe's gaze was intense. 'I need you to come back with me, Charlie, so I can explain everything to you properly. I want us to have another chance. A proper chance.'

Another chance.

Charlie's whole body swayed dizzily. It was just as well Rafe was holding her hands or she might have fallen.

He stepped closer, and she smelled the faintest trace of his cologne as he leaned in to speak softly in her ear. 'I know this is the wrong place and the wrong time, but I've fallen in love with you, Charlie.'

In love. In love. In love.

The words circled in her head, but they felt unreal, like part of a magic spell.

Rafe clasped her hands more tightly. 'Please come back to Montaigne with me.'

Oh-h-h.

She couldn't believe this was happening now.

It was everything she wanted. It was too much to take in. Her poor heart was soaring and swooping like a bird caught in a whirlwind. She longed to lean into Rafe, to be wrapped in his strong arms, to just let him sweep her away.

But she had to be sensible. She had to remember how she'd sat in her room in the early hours of this morning, alone in Rafe's castle, thinking carefully and rationally about everything that had happened between them. She had reminded herself then how very, very easy it was to be blinded by this handsome Prince, by his charm, by his wealth and power.

She knew she had to be super careful now, or she could make a very serious mistake.

Rafe saw the fear in Charlie's pale face and his heart sank. Had he done this to her? Surely he hadn't made her feel so scared? It was the last thing he wanted. 'Charlie, I only want to talk to you, to try to explain.'

She was shaking her head. 'I'm sorry, Rafe. It's too much. Too much pressure.'

'But I wouldn't try to force you into anything.'

'You already have,' she said.

'No, Charlie, I—'

He was silenced by the stubborn light in her eyes. It reminded him of the tough little terrier he'd met in the Sydney art gallery. Right now Charlie looked both tough *and* scared.

'You're trying to get me off this plane, Rafe. What's that if it's not bullying?' Charlie's lovely mouth twisted as if she was trying very hard not to cry.

Again, she shook her head. 'Believe me, I've thought this through properly. We come from totally different worlds. We connected for a couple of days and it was fun. But you were right all along. Happy endings are for dreamers. Real life is all about compromise and common sense.'

Despair ripped through Rafe. He couldn't bear to lose her, to let things end this way.

'Thanks for everything, but I'm going home,' Charlie told him quietly, and then, before he could find the all-important words that might stop her, she turned. Her shoulders were ramrod-straight as she walked back into the plane.

* * *

The flight attendants quickly turned from their whispering huddle when Charlie appeared, but not before she heard snatches of their conversation.

'Rafael...'

'Prince of Montaigne...'

'Playboy...'

She didn't bother to speak to them. With her head high, her eyes stinging but dry, she made the hideously long journey back down the aisle to her seat.

Her large neighbour wasn't happy about having to get out again to let her past. She thanked him and, as soon as she was buckled in her seat, she found the eye mask for sleeping and slipped it on.

Eventually, the huge plane rolled forward on the tarmac, gathering speed, and she told herself over and over that she'd done the right thing, the only sensible thing. She could only hope that if she kept saying this until she reached Sydney, she might at last believe it.

CHAPTER THIRTEEN

Six weeks later

AFTER YET ANOTHER unsuccessful job interview, Charlie climbed the stairs to her flat, lugging grocery bags with food for her cat, as well as the ingredients for her own dinner.

She was now at the end of her second full week of job hunting and she'd lost count of the number of interviews she'd endured. If she'd known it would be this difficult to get another job, she might not have accepted the gallery's redundancy so readily. Not that she'd had much option.

From the moment her father had been heralded as the art world's latest sensation, the directors of the gallery where Charlie had worked for five years had promptly decided to employ experts with 'proper' qualifications. Charlie hadn't been to university, so her intimate knowledge of the work of local artists hadn't counted.

The dismissal had upset her for a day or two.

Her father had protested and wanted to fight for her to stay, but she'd begged him not to cause a fuss. In her heart of hearts, she'd already accepted that it was time to move on. After all, the gallery was a constant reminder of a certain tall, commanding figure who'd come striding through the doors to turn her world upside-down.

Now it was late on a Friday. Charlie reached the landing at the top of the steps and set down her shopping while she fished in her jeans pocket for her keys. It was a warm afternoon at the end of summer. Edna from next door had left her door open to catch a breeze and the smell of her baking wafted down the hallway.

The tempting aroma of freshly baked chocolate cake was accompanied by the sound of voices—Edna's voice and a masculine baritone. Judging by the happy chatter, the two of them were having a jolly old time. Disturbingly, the man's voice reminded Charlie of Rafe's.

So annoying to have yet another reminder of the man she was trying so hard to forget. Pushing the key roughly into the lock, Charlie shoved at the door, holding it open with her knee, while she gathered up the shopping bags.

Meow!

Her darling cat, Dolly, pattered down the hall, eager to greet her. 'Hello, beautiful girl, you're going to love me when you see what I've bought for your dinner.'

Dolly answered with another meow and rubbed her silky black and white body against Charlie's shins. Then she began to sniff at the shopping bags.

Charlie was closing the door when Edna's voice called from the next flat, 'Yoo-hoo! Is that you, Charlie?'

'Yes, Edna, just home.' Charlie tried to inject a little enthusiasm into her response, but she knew from experience that Edna liked to drag her in for a cuppa and to meet her friends. She wasn't in a sociable mood this evening.

If she was honest, she hadn't been in a sociable mood for weeks. A broken heart could do that to a girl, and losing her job hadn't helped. Charlie's dad and her neighbour had both commented on her low moods, but so far they'd been tolerant, sensing that something 'deep' was the cause. However, she knew their tolerance would turn to annoyance before too long.

'Ah,' said Edna's voice.

Charlie turned to see her neighbour beaming from her doorway.

'I told him you should be home soon,' said Edna.

Told *him*?

Charlie's heart began a fretful kind of pounding. 'Told who?' she asked shakily.

Edna's beaming grin broadened. 'Your lovely friend.'

'My—'

Rafe appeared in the hallway behind Edna, and Charlie froze. He was dressed in casual blue jeans and a white T-shirt. His black hair was a little longer and shaggier than she remembered, and his jaw was shadowed by the hint of a beard. He seemed a little leaner and more strained, and yet Charlie thought he'd never looked more gorgeous.

Why was he here?

She had relived the details of their farewell a thousand times, torturing herself with questions about what might have happened if she'd gone with Rafe instead of walking away.

Regrets? Yes, she'd had more than a few, but for the sake of her sanity she'd chosen to believe that she'd done the right thing, the only sensible thing.

Now, amazingly, after six long weeks, here Rafe was. Truly. In the flesh. Charlie was so blindsided she couldn't speak, couldn't think how to react. Could only stand there stupefied.

'Hello, Charlie,' he said.

She might have nodded. She couldn't be sure.

'Rafe told me you weren't expecting him,'

Edna explained self-importantly, almost hugging herself with excitement. 'Isn't this a lovely surprise for you?'

'I—guess,' Charlie muttered faintly.

Her neighbour turned to Rafe. 'Well, I really enjoyed meeting you again, Rafe, and thank you so much for our lovely chat.'

'Thank you for the tea and chocolate cake,' he responded with his customary courtesy.

'I'll leave you two to have a really nice catch-up now.' Edna winked rather obviously at him.

Crikey, thought Charlie. *The poor woman would probably have a heart attack if she knew she was winking so brazenly at a European prince.*

With a final smiling wave, Edna closed her door.

Charlie swallowed as she looked at Rafe. Her impulse was to rush into her flat and slam the door in his face, but that would be childish, not to mention rude. And it would leave her with too many unanswered questions.

Her second thought was to hold Rafe at bay, here on the landing, while she demanded that he explain exactly why he had come all this way. She was still thinking this through when Rafe spoke.

'How's your baby sister?' he asked.

It was the last thing Charlie had expected him

to say and, in an instant, she could feel her resistance crumbling.

'Isla's doing really well,' she said. 'She's home again and she's getting fatter. She even gave her first smile last week.'

'That's wonderful.'

'Yes, it is.' He looked so gorgeous and, with so much emotion shimmering in his eyes, Charlie wanted to hurl herself into his arms. 'I guess you'd better come inside,' she said instead.

'Thank you, Charlie. I'd like that.'

In the hallway, she bent to pick up her shopping.

'Here, let me.' Rafe bent down too and their hands bumped together as they both tried to grab the bags at the same moment.

Lightning flashes engulfed Charlie. She stepped away, her hands clenched to her sides as she thanked him weakly. 'Can you bring the bags through to the kitchen?'

She couldn't believe she was conversing about ordinary everyday things like her shopping bags with Rafe St Romain. Shouldn't she be *demanding* to know exactly why he was here? Why he'd crossed hemispheres to be here?

But those questions felt too huge. Charlie had spent six long weeks trying to get over this man. Unfortunately, she now knew for sure that her efforts had been in vain. The mere sight of him stirred up every last vestige of the old longing and pain.

Oh, help!

Dolly rubbed at her ankles again, meowing more insistently. 'She can smell her dinner,' Charlie said, glad of the distraction. 'I'd better feed her, or she'll drive us mad.'

'By all means.'

She nodded to a red kitchen stool. 'Pull up a pew. Or if you'd prefer, you can sit in the lounge. I won't be long.'

'Here in the kitchen is fine, thanks.'

'Would you like another cup of tea?'

Rafe smiled, rubbed a hand over his flat stomach. 'No, thanks, I'm swimming in tea.'

'Wine?'

He shook his head, and smiled again. 'Take care of your cat.'

Charlie felt as if she'd woken in the middle of a weird dream as she unwrapped the fish she'd bought for Dolly and set it on a chopping board to dice. 'When did you arrive in Sydney, Rafe?'

'A couple of hours ago.'

'You must be feeling jet-lagged.'

'It's not too bad.'

She transferred the fish to Dolly's stainless-steel feeding bowl, set it on the floor, where Dolly greeted it with ecstatic, purring delight.

Rafe laughed. 'That's one happy cat.'

'It's a special treat. Fresh fish is like *foie gras* and champagne for her.' Charlie washed her hands at the sink, dried them on a hand towel hanging on a hook, then turned back to Rafe without quite meeting his gaze. Under normal circumstances she would start cooking her own meal now.

These were anything but normal circumstances.

'I was hoping that you might be free,' Rafe said. 'So I could take you out to dinner tonight.'

'Oh, I—um—' Charlie's head spun dizzily as she imagined dining somewhere glamorous with this man. He would be sure to choose a restaurant with sensational gourmet food, first-class wines, candlelight and ambience by the truckload. She saw herself falling under his spell. Again.

Be careful, girl.

'Actually, I—I was about to cook my dinner,' she told him. 'Why don't you join me here?' She couldn't quite believe she'd said that, but she could hardly send him packing, and surely it was far safer to eat in her kitchen than to go to a restaurant? At least she would be able to keep busy here. She could distract herself with any number of small kitchen tasks.

'There's enough for two,' she said. 'That's if you don't mind a Thai prawn stir-fry?'

Rafe's grey eyes gleamed with an intensity that made her heart stumble. 'Thank you, Charlie. I'd like that very much.'

She swallowed. Now she felt stupidly nervous about cooking a meal in front of this Prince, even though she'd made the dish so many times she could practically do it in her sleep.

'What can I do to help?' Rafe asked.

She blinked at him. 'Do you know how to cook? Have you ever been in a kitchen?'

He smiled. 'Not since I was a small boy, but I used to love sneaking downstairs to help the cooks to peel apples, or to cut out gingerbread men.'

It was an endearing thought, and, despite her qualms, Charlie set two chopping boards and two knives on the counter. 'You can help with chopping the veggies, then. I'll do the onions—I'd hate to see a grown man cry. You can do the carrots. Or would you prefer—?'

'Carrots are fine.'

It was surreal. Six weeks ago, they had parted at the door of an international jet amidst a huge amount of embarrassment and tension and now there were still huge questions hanging in the air. But Rafe seemed perfectly happy to help with preparing their dinner as if they were an old couple who'd lived harmoniously together for ages.

Charlie showed him how to cut carrots on the diagonal for stir-frying, rather than in strips or rounds.

'Stir-frying needs to be very quick and this way there's more of the carrot's surface area coming in contact with the heat.'

He nodded. 'That makes sense.'

As they chopped capsicum, shallots and fresh ginger Charlie asked about Tobias and Mathilde, Guillaume and Chloe. Rafe told her they were all well.

He looked up from his task, sending her a glance that hinted at amusement. 'They all asked to be remembered to you.'

'Oh.' This was a surprise. Her face flamed as she nipped the ends off snow peas, and she refrained from asking any more questions as she set jasmine rice cooking on a back burner.

Charlie found the fish sauce she needed and combined it with soy sauce, sesame oil and honey in a small bowl. Luckily the prawns were already peeled, so she could avoid that messy task.

As she set the wok on the gas flame she wondered what Rafe was *really* thinking. She felt tense as a bowstring. Questions kept popping into her head, but they were so very personal and important that to ask them felt as reckless as running through a field of unexploded landmines.

She forced herself to concentrate on her task, working calmly and methodically, cooking the prawns in the hot oil with garlic and chilli.

'When do the vegetables go in?' Rafe asked as he came to stand beside her.

'Soon. They only take a few minutes.'

'It smells sensational.'

Her skin was flaming—not from the cooking heat, but from his proximity. 'Would you—ah—mind setting the table? The plates and bowls are in the cupboard up there.' She pointed. 'And the cutlery's in that drawer.'

Rafe set the table with black place mats and white china and Charlie's red-handled cutlery, while Charlie transferred the stir-fry and the rice into two black and white ceramic bowls.

'Wine!' she announced. She suddenly, most definitely, needed wine. 'There's a nice cold white chilling in the fridge. I'll get the glasses.'

But she'd run out of delaying tactics. In a matter of moments, everything was ready. Rafe was sitting opposite her at her dining table, and he was smiling—looking unaccountably happy, actually—and drop-dead sexy in his casual jeans and T-shirt. And Charlie knew her efforts to keep herself busy and diverted had been no help whatsoever.

Even without the glamour of a fancy restaurant and mood lighting, even here in her ordinary little flat with a simple home-cooked meal, Prince Rafael of Montaigne was as attractive and charming as ever. And she was still totally, hopelessly under his spell.

Worse, she knew they could no longer avoid the important conversations they'd been dancing around, although Rafe seemed in no hurry to broach them.

'This is delicious,' he said. 'The flavours are fantastic.'

'I'm glad you like it.' The meal wasn't exactly flash.

'I love it, Charlie. This is exactly what I hoped for.'

'Prawn stir-fry?'

He chuckled. 'To see you in your natural environment.'

'You make me sound like some kind of rare animal.'

'Sorry.' He gave a dismayed shake of his head. 'Am I making a hash of this?'

Was he? Charlie thought he was being rather lovely, just as he'd been in Montaigne, although she was still uncertain and confused about the purpose of his surprise visit.

'You were right,' Rafe said suddenly, after he'd helped himself to another spoonful of veggies. 'I should never have tried to drag you off that plane. I was an egotistical bully. I realised that, as soon as you turned and walked away from me. I couldn't believe I'd been so crass.'

He looked so repentant, the final wedge of resistance in Charlie's heart melted.

'I shouldn't have run away,' she admitted. 'I should have at least stayed at the castle until I'd thanked you for your wonderful hospitality. I should have said goodbye properly.'

Rafe shrugged. 'I couldn't really blame you for rushing off. You'd been through the wringer. I'd dragged you across the world and you had the stress of trying to pretend to be someone else. Not to mention all the worry about your little sister.'

'And I also had a certain playboy prince kissing me senseless when he wasn't supposed to.'

The smoulder in Rafe's eyes sent Charlie's skin flaming again. 'I'm not going to apologise for kissing you.'

The air seemed to crackle with the chemistry sparking between them. Charlie dropped her gaze. 'It was pretty awkward to have Olivia turning up just at that moment—'

'It was,' Rafe agreed. 'Her timing was uncanny.'

He set down his fork. To Charlie's surprise, he smiled and leaned back in his chair, looking totally relaxed.

'So how is Montaigne's political situation

now?' she asked, having deliberately avoided searching the Internet for news of his country. It had seemed sensible to try to put the whole experience behind her, but now, with Rafe here in her flat, dining at her table, she needed to get her facts straight before her brain went into total meltdown. 'Is everything settled?'

Rafe nodded. 'Our new Chancellor is brilliant. Leroy Mining have pulled in their horns. Everything's back to the way it should be as far as I'm concerned.'

'That must be a relief. And where's Olivia these days?'

'On her honeymoon, I imagine.'

Charlie's eyes widened. 'She's married already? To her fellow in Monaco?'

'Yes. His name's Frederick Hugo.' Rafe took a lazy sip of his wine. 'And she has also spilled her story to the press.'

'About you—and—'

'And about you,' Rafe supplied smoothly. 'Olivia's big reveal. It was a double-page spread in a really popular glossy. Everything out in the open about how she only became engaged to me to help Montaigne, and the real love of her life was Frederick.'

'Gosh.'

Rafe didn't look the slightest bit put out. 'No doubt the magazine paid her a fortune. That's fine.' He smiled. 'She's saved me from having to explain how there came to be two of you.'

Charlie swallowed. 'So that's in the magazines, too? About Olivia and me being identical twins?'

'Yes, including photos of you at the hospital. Olivia declared she was ever so grateful that her sister stepped in when she had her little crisis.'

'So now your whole country knows who I really am?'

'Well, those who read gossip magazines, at any rate. But it means,' Rafe added carefully, 'that if you ever wanted to come back to Montaigne, we wouldn't have to worry about awkward explanations.'

'I—I see.'

'Of course,' he added, 'I'm being plagued with questions about you, especially about why I let you go.'

Charlie found this hard to believe. 'Who would ask about me?'

Rafe smiled again. 'Absolutely everyone. My staff. My good friend Faysal. Monique at Belle Robe. The people at the hospital. Just about anyone who's met you, Charlie.'

She had no idea what to say to this. She was astonished that these people even remembered her, let alone cared about her. Totally flustered, she stood abruptly and wondered if it was too soon to start clearing the table.

Rafe stood too and he moved towards her, reached for her hand before she could try to pick up a plate.

'Charlie,' he said softly.

'What?' She could barely hear her nervous response above the thumping of her heart.

'You were right to be cautious. We do hardly know each other.' His hand closed around hers. 'But I meant what I said at the airport. I want us to have a second chance.'

A second chance...

Charlie was as enchanted by Rafe's touch, by the pressure of his fingers wrapped around hers, as she was by his words. But there were things she needed to sort out. This man was supposed to be finding himself a wife to help him to rule Montaigne. He had access to the wealthiest and most beautiful women in Europe and he now had time to court one of these women properly. So what was he doing in a suburban flat in Sydney?

'What sort of second chance are we talking about, Rafe? Last time you wanted me to pretend to be your fiancée.'

'I know, I know.' He gave a soft groan. 'Looking back it was crazy, but it was the best crazy thing I've ever done.'

Now he reached for her other hand and held them both together, cradled against his chest.

Charlie could feel the heat of him through his thin white T-shirt, feel the thud of his heartbeats. She blinked back tears and tried to breathe. *Don't cry. Not now.*

'Charlie, I've missed you so much I thought I was going out of my mind.'

She couldn't speak. All the air had been sucked out of her lungs.

'But I owe it to you to do better,' Rafe said. 'I want us to go about dating the way any other couple might. No pressure, no huge expectations. Just the two of us getting to know each other, seeing how things work out.'

'Where—where might this happen?'

'Here. In Sydney.'

'You mean, you'd stay here in Sydney?'

'For a while, a couple of weeks at least. I'd love to explore this place with you. Bondi Beach, the harbour, maybe the Blue Mountains.'

It was Charlie's idea of bliss and she could no longer think of reasonable objections. 'Well, I don't happen to have a job any more, so I'm actually free.'

'That's handy.' Laughter shone in Rafe's eyes.

Charlie tried to smile back at him, but she couldn't see him now for tears.

It didn't matter. Rafe's arms were around her.

Strong and reassuring and safe. She closed her eyes, let her head rest against his chest. It felt like coming home.

He didn't kiss her immediately. For long lovely moments he just held her close as if she was the most precious thing in the world. And when his lips finally found hers, his kiss was lazy and lingering, and the magic was there from the first contact.

Charlie felt the heat and the power of him flowing through her, touching flashpoints, igniting the yearning that had never really gone away.

Rafe in jeans and a T-shirt, here in Australia, was every bit as sexy and dangerous as he'd been in his castle in full princely regalia. Desire curled through Charlie like smoke. Like smoke and flames and she wanted to press close to him, to wriggle against him, to tear off her clothes.

Between increasingly frantic kisses, she asked, 'Have you booked into a hotel?'

'Yes. Somewhere near the harbour.'

'But you said you wanted to see me in my natural environment.'

Rafe smiled. 'That's true, I do.'

'Then you should cancel your booking,' she suggested recklessly. 'Stay here.'

She heard the sharp rasp of his breath. 'That would be perfect.'

Then in a burst of unbelievable confidence, she said, 'But, of course, you'd need to check my bedroom first. Make sure the mattress is up to scratch.'

Now he laughed. 'Have I ever told you I love the way you think, Charlie girl?'

In one easy motion he swept her high, holding her with an arm beneath her knees and another around her shoulders. 'Which way is the bedroom?'

Charlie pointed.

Of course, she knew she should be nervous about directing a royal prince to her boudoir. She had no idea what happened when a girl let a fairy tale and real life collide. But she was too entranced to analyse the problem, too impressed by Rafe's strength, by the easy way he carried her as if she were a featherweight.

'It's like a glamorous cave in here,' he said as he set her down on the snowy white bed in her black-walled bedroom with just a single lamp glowing in the corner.

'I got carried away with the black and white theme.'

'It's great. I love it.' He sat on the bed beside her, and her body hummed with anticipation as he leaned over her, supporting himself with a hand on the mattress on either side of her.

Please, she whispered silently. She'd never felt so ready, so wanting.

Bending closer, he kissed her throat, her chin, her brow and, in that moment, as her eyes drifted closed, he pressed gentle kisses to her eyelids, and Charlie forgot the whole prince thing. This was Rafe and that was all that mattered. Rafe, the hunkiest *and* the nicest guy she'd ever met, who'd come all this way to get to know her.

'I've missed you so much I thought I was going out of my mind,' he'd said.

He kissed her mouth, teasing her lips apart with his tongue, and any last efforts to think dissolved as sensation claimed her, washing over her in heated, hungry waves. She wound her arms around his neck, and her hips bucked, needing him closer still.

It should have been gentle and lingering, this first time, but they'd been waiting too long. Need built fast and furiously, breaking through any final barriers of politeness. Everything went a little wild and slightly desperate as they helped each other out of their clothes and then scrambled to be close again. Skin to skin.

At the centre of the wildness there was happiness, too. For Charlie, a fierce, bubbling, over-the-top joy. She and the man who'd stolen her heart were together at last, and everything was OK. It was perfect.

* * *

It was ten days later when Charlie got the phone call. For Rafe they had been ten glorious days, spent exclusively with Charlie, exploring Sydney, dining out, cooking at home, talking, talking, making love. A kind of honeymoon without the wedding. A perfection they both knew couldn't last.

On this particular day they had been to the Blue Mountains, hiking, checking out the gift shops and dining in a hotel with an amazing view of craggy cliffs and a deep, tree-studded valley. Rafe was driving his hire car back into Charlie's garage when her phone rang. She had to fish the phone out of her bag.

'I've no idea who this can be,' she said as she checked the caller ID. She climbed out of the car to answer the call.

Rafe collected their sweaters from the back seat, locked the car, and indicated to Charlie that he would go ahead to open the flat.

Still intent on the phone conversation, she nodded.

He was in the kitchen, giving Dolly a welcome scratch behind her ears, when Charlie came in. Charlie's eyes were wide, as if she'd had a shock, but there was also a tightness in her expressive face that suggested she might not want to share her news.

'That was unexpected,' she said, setting her phone on the kitchen counter.

'Is everything OK?' Rafe asked cautiously.

'Well, I guess. I've been offered a job.'

An unwelcome chill spread over his skin. Charlie had already told him about her father's sudden rise to fame and the changes at the art gallery where she used to work. But they hadn't talked about her future plans. They'd been busy making the most of their time together, and Rafe had promised Charlie there would be no pressure or expectation, so he'd been careful to hold any discussion about the future at bay. Charlie hadn't mentioned any job prospects.

'It's weird,' she said now. 'I've applied for all kinds of positions and been knocked back and now I'm offered a job I never even applied for.'

Rafe's throat tightened. 'What kind of offer?'

'To run another art gallery at the Gold Coast. In Queensland.' Her eyes widened and it was clear she was impressed. 'There's a big tourist market up there,' she said. 'A huge turnover.'

'A big responsibility, then.' Rafe spoke quietly, despite the chilling lump of dread that had settled in his gut.

Now he regretted his reticence to talk about their future. He hadn't wanted to rush Charlie, to overwhelm her with the truth about his deep feelings for her. But the past days had only served to prove to him how important she was to him.

In every way, Charlie was the most desirable woman he'd ever known, but his feelings went way beyond their incredible chemistry. With her own special brand of wisdom, Charlie brought the perfect balance to his world.

As he juggled the privileges of royalty with its responsibilities, he needed this sunny, open-hearted and genuine girl in his life. By his side.

Hell. Had he left it too late?

Charlie stood very still with her arms folded tightly over her chest, trying hard not to mind that Rafe had taken her news so calmly, as if he wasn't in any way a part of her future.

A big responsibility, then.

Was that all he could say?

After ten of the best days of her life? After ten ecstatically beautiful days filled with fun and laughter and their deepening friendship, not to mention sublimely satisfying sex?

Foolishly, she'd spent these ten days falling more deeply and helplessly in love with the man, despite the fact that there'd been no talk at all about where any of this was leading.

Now Charlie hugged herself tighter and tried not to panic. But Rafe was taking her news so calmly. Too calmly. Had she been a total fool?

Had she totally misunderstood where their relationship was heading?

Was the new job opportunity a turning point? Was Rafe about to gently let her go?

It was really nice knowing you, Charlie, but I'm royalty after all, and I'm afraid you're not quite up to scratch.

'I didn't realise you were still job-hunting,' Rafe said.

Charlie shrugged miserably and kept her gaze on the black and white floor tiles. 'I wasn't really hunting for this job.'

'If I'd known you were looking for work, I might have spoken earlier,' he said. 'I'd like to offer you a job.'

She stiffened. A job offer from Rafe was like a slap in the face. What did he have in mind? To employ her as some kind of secretary-cum-mistress?

How dared he?

'No, thanks,' she snapped, jamming her lips tightly together to bite back the sob that threatened.

'Because being my wife is a kind of job, I'm afraid.'

At first, Charlie thought she'd misheard him.

'As you know,' Rafe went on with uncharacteristic earnestness, 'there are certain expectations and responsibilities. But I think—no, I don't just think, I *know* you'd be brilliant at that particular job, Charlie. So I was hoping you'd do me the honour—'

He stopped talking and looked at her with a smile that was both shy and hopeful.

Charlie stopped hugging herself. Instead she gripped the counter before her knees gave way. 'I'm sorry,' she said shakily. 'I think I might have missed something. What exactly are you asking me?'

And that was when it happened. Tall, impossibly handsome Rafael St Romain, Prince of Montaigne, got down on one knee on her kitchen floor and placed a hand over his heart.

'I love you, Charlie. I suspect I've been in love with you from the day I first met you, but now I know it for certain and it's a relief to be able to tell you at last.'

Oh.

'I'm desperate to spend the rest of my life with you.'

'Oh-h-h-h.'

'And I'm shamelessly begging you to marry me.'

'Oh, Rafe.' Charlie dashed at tears with one hand while she held her other hand out to him. 'I've been the same.' Her voice was very wobbly as she linked her fingers with his. 'I didn't know it was possible to love someone so deeply. I had no idea till I met you.'

The intensity in his face was heart-stopping. 'So you'll marry me?'

Charlie was grinning now, with tears streaming down her face. 'Only if you get up off that floor and kiss me.'

Leaping to his feet, Rafe was more than happy to oblige. 'I promise I'll make you happy,' he said as he gathered Charlie close.

'And if marrying you is a job, my first job will be to keep you happy, too,' she told him.

A pleading meow sounded at their feet. Charlie felt a silken pressure against her ankles and looked down to a swishing black and white tail. 'Oh, dear. If we get married, what will happen to Dolly?'

Rafe smiled. 'No worries, as you Aussies say. She'll fit in just fine in the castle.'

And then he kissed her and, despite the thousand wonderful kisses they'd shared, this was the very best kiss of all.

EPILOGUE

THE BELLS RANG LOUDLY, pealing from churches all over Montaigne, echoing from the mountainsides and rolling down the valleys. Loudest of all were the bells from the cathedral where Prince Rafael and his bride, Princess Charlotte, were to be married.

The joyful sounds surrounded Charlie and her dad as they drove through the streets, lined with crowds of cheering well-wishers who were waving flags or homemade signs.

We love you, Charlie!
Bonne chance!
Félicitations!

Charlie couldn't help being overwhelmed by all the excitement and goodwill. She felt quite nervous by the time she and her father arrived at the cathedral and the bells were replaced by thundering organ music, lifting to the magnificent soaring ceilings.

Is this real? Is this really happening to me?

As she stood in the enormous cathedral doorway, Charlie trembled as she saw the splendour of it all—the stained-glass windows, the candles, the bishop in his robes, the pews filled with grand-looking strangers. She was almost too scared to look properly at Rafe, who stood at the far end of the very long aisle, incredibly splendid in a red jacket with gold braid and black trousers. She was so overcome she feared she might weep.

In that moment, however, her eye was caught by a bobbing flash of deep purple right at the front of the congregation. Someone had turned to grin and to wave excitedly. Charlie realised it was Edna.

Her neighbour had been over the moon to be invited to the royal wedding and today she looked magnificent in a purple lace suit, with a lavender fascinator, complete with feathers, perched rather precariously on her head.

The sight of her old neighbour's familiar beaming grin was enough to calm Charlie.

She looked again at Rafe. And he smiled.

His smile was for her. Only for her. She could feel his love reaching her down the full length of the red-carpeted aisle, and she knew that, despite the over-the-top pomp and ceremony, Rafe was just a normal guy who needed her.

He had told her this over and over during the past few days.

They loved each other. They might be a royal couple, but they were also good mates. Everything was OK.

With a happy, calming, deep breath, Charlie turned her attention to Arielle, her flower girl, who had just arrived in the car that followed close behind.

Arielle was one of the first people Charlie had visited on her return to Montaigne. The little girl's hair had grown back since the day they'd first met in the hospital, when she'd worn a crocheted cap and had won Rafe and Charlie's hearts with her curtsy. On Charlie's second visit, she had met Arielle's parents as well. Since then her friendship with the family and with many other patients had deepened.

Today the excited little girl looked beautiful with her mop of short dark curls adorned by a circlet of roses that matched her floor-length dress of palest pink. Olivia looked beautiful too in a gown in the same shade. She'd been thrilled and touched when Charlie had invited her to be her matron of honour.

And Suze, Charlie's best friend since kindergarten, was also a bridesmaid, looking perfectly lovely, but slightly overawed by the fact that her groomsman partner was a handsome sheikh.

Now, with everyone assembled, Charlie sent them all a final smile and then linked arms with her dad. Michael Morisset had taken a while to get used to the idea of his daughter marrying a prince. At first he'd thought Charlie was pulling his leg. It was too preposterous to believe.

Fortunately, once he'd got to know Rafe, he'd calmed down. Eventually, he'd declared his prospective son-in-law to be a regular 'good bloke'.

'I was worried Rafe wouldn't understand how lucky he was,' Charlie's father had confided. 'But he seems to truly appreciate how wonderful you are, my duckling, so I'm happy to give you my blessing.'

Now her dad smiled at her. His eyes were a tad too shiny, but he still looked happy. 'I'm so proud of you, kiddo,' he said fondly, a beat before the organist struck the opening chords of the processional hymn.

The congregation rose, the music swelled and flowed, and Charlie kept her smile just for Rafe as she made her way down the long, long aisle. Throughout the procession, her Prince didn't take his eyes from her and his message was clear and shining.

This day wasn't just a happy ending, it was the very happiest of new beginnings.

* * * * *

If you loved this story and want to enjoy another wedding romance look out for SLOW DANCE WITH THE BEST MAN by Sophie Pembroke.

If you love nothing more than a Cinderella story you won't want to miss Therese Beharrie's fabulous debut book THE TYCOON'S RELUCTANT CINDERELLA!

COMING NEXT MONTH FROM

HARLEQUIN® *Romance*

Available February 7, 2017

#4555 THE SHEIKH'S CONVENIENT PRINCESS

Romantic Getaways • by Liz Fielding

To reconcile with his estranged father, Sheikh Ibrahim al-Ansari must find a bride! Luckily he has the perfect convenient princess in mind—his new assistant, Ruby Dance. Ruby agrees to a temporary marriage, but soon she can't help craving the devastating beauty of the desert and the man who rules it...

#4556 THE UNFORGETTABLE SPANISH TYCOON

Romantic Getaways • by Christy McKellen

Once, Elena Jones shared an intense entanglement with striking Spaniard Caleb Araya, but it ended with both their hearts in tatters. When a sudden accident means the tycoon remembers nothing, Elena seizes the chance to make things right. But the closer they get, the more Elena realizes her own heart has never forgotten him...

#4557 THE BILLIONAIRE OF CORAL BAY

Romantic Getaways • by Nikki Logan

When gorgeous Richard Grundy arrives in Coral Bay, he sends Mila Nakano's senses into overdrive. The secret billionaire prides himself on making decisions with his head...until he's captivated by gentle, exotic Mila! Now he has the toughest job yet: persuading her to be Coral Bay's newest bride!

#4558 HER FIRST-DATE HONEYMOON

Romantic Getaways

by Katrina Cudmore

Runaway bride Emma Fox is determined to gain her independence by using her would-be honeymoon in Venice to secure a temporary job with billionaire Matteo Vieri. Working together in his palazzo warms Matteo's guarded heart... They've already shared a honeymoon, but will he ask Emma to walk down the aisle?

YOU CAN FIND MORE INFORMATION ON UPCOMING HARLEQUIN® TITLES, FREE EXCERPTS AND MORE AT WWW.HARLEQUIN.COM.

HRLPCNM0117

Sheikh Ibrahim al-Ansari must find a bride, and quickly... Thankfully he has the perfect convenient princess in mind—his new assistant, Ruby Dance!

Read on for a sneak preview of
THE SHEIKH'S CONVENIENT PRINCESS
by Liz Fielding.

"Can I ask if you are in any kind of relationship?" he persisted.

"Relationship?"

"You are on your own—you have no ties?"

He was beginning to spook her and must have realized it because he said, "I have a proposition for you, Ruby, but if you have personal commitments..." He shook his head as if he wasn't sure what he was doing.

"If you're going to offer me a package too good to refuse after a couple of hours I should warn you that it took Jude Radcliffe the best part of a year to get to that point and I still turned him down."

"I don't have the luxury of time," he said, "and the position I'm offering is made for a temp."

"I'm listening."

"Since you have done your research, you know that I was disinherited five years ago."

She nodded. She thought it rather harsh for a one-off incident but the media loved the fall of a hero and had gone into a bit of a feeding frenzy.

"This morning I received a summons from my father to present myself at his birthday majlis."

"You can go home?"

"If only it were that simple. A situation exists, which means that I can only return to Umm al Basr if I'm accompanied by a wife."

She ignored the slight sinking feeling in her stomach. Obviously a multimillionaire who looked like the statue of a Greek god—albeit one who'd suffered a bit of wear and tear—would have someone ready and willing to step up to the plate.

"That's rather short notice. Obviously, I'll do whatever I can to arrange things, but I don't know a lot about the law in—"

"The marriage can take place tomorrow. My question is, under the terms of your open-ended brief encompassing 'whatever is necessary,' are you prepared to take on the role?"

Make sure to read...
THE SHEIKH'S CONVENIENT PRINCESS
by Liz Fielding.

Available February 2017 wherever
Harlequin® Romance books and ebooks are sold.

www.Harlequin.com

HREXP0117